THE SCARIEST TAIL

A Wonder Cats Mystery Book 4

HARPER LIN

ISBN-13: 978-1987859317

ISBN-10: 1987859316

www.harperlin.com

John Roy

❧❦❧

Contrary to popular belief, witches rarely stare into bubbling cauldrons of smoky liquid in order to see what is going on in the world. Movies and books might show a lot of that, but we actually get most of our information the old-fashioned way: through neighborhood gossip.

My Aunt Astrid is the only one of us witches in the Greenstone family who can actually see the future. But even she has to rely on the universe to decide what she should see and when. For example, she wouldn't know when a person is going to die, but she can predict a nasty fall on some ice this upcoming winter. Slipping in and out of dimensions is second nature to her—as easy as slipping on ice, I suppose.

Most people think she is just an old hippie who saw one too many Grateful Dead concerts. Wild, graying hair hangs in lovely tendrils around her face, and she always wears gypsy skirts and blouses. Sometimes, Aunt Astrid will just be staring into space, and people will think she's zoning out.

The truth is, she's watching something happen in a parallel universe. Sometimes it's important. Sometimes it's just amusing. Sometimes it's downright scary, like it was this particular Thursday when we were all at Bea's house for dinner.

Bea is my cousin. She and I have been the best of friends since Aunt Astrid adopted me after my parents died. I had a normal childhood as far as I was concerned, but I missed my parents. I still do. If it weren't for Bea and her special talent, well, I shudder to think of what might have happened to me.

All the Greenstone women are witches. Our paranormal lineage predates the Salem Witch Trials by at least a couple hundred years. I'm not trying to brag, but we are sort of like witchcraft royalty... except that no one knows we are witches.

I blame Hollywood. Whether it is seeing the future, communicating with the dead, or manipulating the weather, these are gifts no witch asked for.

We were just born with them. But the movies and television have us running around naked in the woods, sacrificing children and animals, or even worse, we are portrayed as dingbat beauty queens who ask permission to take a leaf off a tree. Yikes. We are nothing like that. Posers might be like that, wearing black all the time and carrying around Anton LeVay's satanic bible, but real witches are good.

The Greenstones have taken a vow to keep our special talents secret and only use them for good. I have to admit that is sometimes hard for a person like me who would love to have tossed a pimple spell or flatulence curse on one or two people I've experienced in my lifetime. Like Darla Castellan. She's been my sworn enemy since high school, and I just can't say enough bad things about her. But this story isn't about Darla. It's about something much, much worse. I didn't know such a thing even existed, but I learned Darla was an evil easily controlled. There are things out there, darker things, that can't be.

"I'M NOT SAYING I DON'T LIKE YOUR meatloaf," I argued with my cousin Bea.

"I told you, it isn't meat," she said. "It's a mushroom loaf with half a dozen exotic mushrooms. You didn't even notice the difference."

Once a month for the last several years, my cousin Bea has had Aunt Astrid and me over to her house for dinner. We all lived on the same block. I lived in the little white house with black shutters. Bea and her husband Jake lived five houses down in the lovely two-story yellow house. Across the street between our two houses was the fabulous brownstone with stained glass windows in which Bea's mother, my Aunt Astrid, lived.

"I did notice the difference," I said to Bea. "I knew this wasn't meat. I just didn't want to say anything in case this wasn't how it was supposed to turn out."

I always teased Bea about her cooking but only because I admired what she could do with a can of beans and some homemade chicken stock. She insisted on eating healthy.

She smiled from across her kitchen island. "It doesn't hurt you to eat something that isn't greasy for a change."

"What are you talking about? I brought the salad." I had to defend myself from her vegan bombardment.

"It's taco salad."

I started to laugh. "Yes, but as you can see, there is very little meat. It's mostly beans."

"Great." Bea laughed. "That will be pleasant later on tonight when we're playing Scrabble."

Even Aunt Astrid cracked up at that one.

Once I regained my composure, I assured Bea that I did indeed like her mushroom loaf. It was actually very delicious and certainly better than the peanut-butter-and-jelly sandwich I would have prepared for myself if I'd been alone at home. I was pretty sure that one of the reasons Bea had us over for dinner was to make sure I had vegetables in my meal at least once a month.

Bea was a health nut and was convinced that a healthy body attracted healthy energy. She could see when she touched people whether or not their energy was helping or hindering them. So on top of creating healthy and tasty treats for us at home, she shared the positive mojo through her special teas, coffees, and food that were served at the Brew-Ha-Ha Café where we all worked together six days a week.

Just then, I felt a warm fuzziness around my ankle. Looking down, I was happy to see the golden fur of Peanut Butter, Bea's cat.

"Meow," he blurted out.

"*Where is your buddy, Marshmallow?*" I asked tele-pathically.

"*She's on the ledge in the window, looking out front,*" Peanut Butter replied back to me. "*I think I heard some scratching in the wall by the closet. I'm going to sit there.*" Leaving my side, he went to go inspect the myste-rious scratching.

"*If you catch the mouse, make sure to leave it in Jake's slipper,*" I said to him, chuckling to myself.

I could talk to animals. Cats seemed to be the easiest for me to communicate with, but I could get into a good conversation with just about anything that walked on four legs. In fact, I often thought I was better at communicating exactly what I meant to my furry friends than I ever could to the majority of the human race.

Marshmallow was Aunt Astrid's cat. She was older and super powerful just like Aunt Astrid. At that moment, Marshmallow appeared in the hallway just outside the kitchen. She looked at me with dreamy, half-closed eyes.

"*Did I hear my name?*" She sat down on her back legs and began to groom.

"*Just wondering where you were. Is there anything happening outside?*" I asked.

Marshmallow yawned. I took that as a no.

We finished our meal of mushroom loaf with taco salad, and we were just about to start our board game and dig into the fresh-baked apple pie Aunt Astrid had made when the lights of a car pulling into the driveway flashed past the windows. Jake was home.

"He's home a bit early, isn't he?" Aunt Astrid asked, looking at her watch.

"Must have been a slow night." Bea pulled a plate down from her cupboard and sliced a thick piece of mushroom loaf then popped it in the microwave.

"Don't forget to give him some salad," I said, winking at my cousin.

I heard the front door open and Jake's footsteps start toward the kitchen. Then the footsteps stopped, went back toward the door, then turned and came back toward where we were sitting. I felt something shift in the air. Jake wasn't home because it was a slow night. On the contrary, something had happened.

Finally, he stepped into the kitchen and stood for just a second in the doorway. Bea had her back to him as she fiddled with the microwave door.

"Hey, honey," Bea said. "They let you guys out a

little early?" She turned and looked at him. "Jake? What's the matter?"

When I looked at him, the first thing that popped into my mind was that something bad had happened to his partner Blake Samberg. I would never verbalize that thought, not in a million years. But for a few terrifying seconds, I thought maybe Blake had been hurt or worse.

Blake Samberg was the latest addition to the Wonder Falls Police Department, and he was a no-nonsense, just-the-facts-ma'am, you-can't-handle-the-truth kind of detective. He was also rude, especially to me. But he had the most handsome face—intense dark eyes framed with thick eyebrows. His shoulders were straight and square as though they could support a barn ceiling. Too bad he felt the need to continually tell me I was wrong in every aspect of life, from parking my car to walking at night to washing dishes.

I had seen him on a few occasions when he was in interrogation mode, and he seemed to be the yang to the kind and patient good-cop, Jake. That was probably why they made such a good team.

So I held my breath as Jake came in slowly. Since I was closest to him, I stood up so he could sit on the stool where I'd been perched. Going to the fridge, I pulled out a bottle of water and handed it to him.

"I'm all right," he said, almost as though the words were confusing.

Oh, no. It is Blake.

"Where is Blake?" Aunt Astrid asked as if reading my mind. I looked at her a little suspiciously, but she just watched Jake.

"He's radioing in that we're here. He'll be in in a minute." Jake took another swallow of water, and I let my breath out, hopeful no one had noticed.

Just then, I heard the front door squeak open and shut. Solid, loud, confident footsteps marched along the hardwood floor and into the kitchen. Blake nodded his greeting and stepped up to the island.

"Hello, Blake. It's so nice to see you." Aunt Astrid gave him a hug and offered him her seat.

"Nice to see you too, Astrid. Please, no. I'm fine."

Whatever had happened seemed to take its toll on Jake, but Blake seemed relatively in control of himself. I went to the fridge, grabbed him a bottle of water, and without a word, handed it to him. He reached out and took it, his eyes locking on mine, and I felt a blush coming on. Quickly, I turned away, walking around the island and pulling a few more plates down for the guys to have some apple pie.

By the time I turned back around, I could feel my cheeks were no longer red.

"Bea," Jake began, "do you remember John Roy?"

Bea looked up to the ceiling for a moment. "John Roy? The name sounds familiar, but I can't nail it down."

"He was on the softball team, remember? Kind of balding, a bit on the pudgy side but real nice. He had that wife with the blond hair."

Bea began to nod her head. "Oh, yeah. Yeah, she was a really nice woman. She wrote children's books, didn't she?"

"Yeah. And he was a lawyer," Jake said, his face becoming grave.

"Why? What happened?"

"He killed himself today."

Urban Legend

✦✦✦

"What?" Bea asked, clutching her throat.

"Oh, no." Aunt Astrid sadly shook her head.

I just watched. I didn't know the man or his wife, but suicides always bothered me. Maybe I was troubled because I knew there was almost always something else at play that motivated a person to do such a thing. Or maybe it was because I just hated to think of the pain and loss always left in the wake of such an action. Obviously, it had bothered Jake.

"Did he leave a note?" Bea asked the only hopeful question to which the answer was almost always no.

"We don't know yet. His wife, Lisa, was inconsolable. We didn't have a chance to interview her." Jake took another drink of water. "I just don't get it. He was a really nice guy. I mean, they lived in Prestwick, not a cheap part of town. He had a good job and a pretty wife and was always in a good mood whenever I saw him. It doesn't make any sense."

"Prestwick?" I asked. "Darla Castellan lives there. Maybe he spoke with her."

All heads turned and looked at me.

"What?" was all I could ask.

"No," Jake said. "They lived in the same neighborhood but at opposite ends."

Bea rubbed Jake's hand. "Honey, I am so sorry. Are you hungry at all?"

"Not really," Jake replied.

"I could use a bite." Blake raised his right hand to get Bea's attention.

"Of course, Blake." Bea smiled. "Cath, get Blake some silverware. We had mushroom loaf. It's like meatloaf, only with mushrooms and a thick brown gravy." She set the plate she had heated in front of Blake, who dug right in.

"Tastes wonderful," Blake said. "Do you use oregano?"

"I used just a pinch with old-fashioned salt and pepper."

"Next time, may I suggest a little cilantro instead of the oregano? Not a lot because it can be overwhelming but maybe a teaspoon. You'd be surprised."

I rolled my eyes.

"That does sound good." Bea nodded. "That might be something for the café."

I looked at Jake, who was busy studying the droplets of water that had formed on the outside of the bottle he was holding.

Stepping a little closer to him, I put my hand on his. "You okay?"

He looked at me and smiled.

Jake was the big brother I never had. I was thrilled when he and Bea got married, and after some rocky terrain and a few harsh words, the two of them were really dedicated to each other.

Jake was the only outsider who knew we were all witches. He didn't know the extent of our powers. Once or twice, he had seen Bea in action, and he realized how lucky he was to be with her. Plus, he was the only other person besides me who didn't think the Scrabble board was relegated to polite words only. Poop was a word too.

"Yeah, Cath. I'm okay." He took a deep breath. "But did you ever get the feeling that there is something headed your way, but you didn't know what it was or when it would get here?"

"Sometimes," I said.

"That's how I feel." He looked sad, but when he looked at Bea, his face brightened a little. She had that kind of soothing effect. "Bea, I'm going to go upstairs and take a shower."

"Good idea, honey. Would you like some tea?"

"That would be nice. Thanks. Ladies, Blake, if you'll excuse me."

Before Jake could make his way up the stairs, Blake followed him into the hallway where they were out of earshot. Peanut Butter sat there, still listening for the scratching inside the wall.

"Hey!" I called to him in my mind. *"What are the guys talking about?"*

Peanut Butter looked at me then up at the men who were right in front of him. *"Um, something about getting the whole story. Something about not panicking, and that kind of stuff isn't true... an urban legend."*

Peanut Butter then stood up, stretched his muscles, and strolled my way, only he avoided me altogether and went to lie on the grate in the corner of the kitchen where the warm air came up from the furnace.

It was early October, and the leaves were just starting to change. The heat was kicking on more frequently, and the skies were grayer than usual. I loved it. Cold weather suited me better than a bathing suit ever did. If the temps required big, bulky sweaters and boots, then I was happy.

But the other things that happened in October could get a bit out of hand. On the paranormal front, there was no denying that things became more active. A suicide in town could have had something to do with the time of year, or it might just have been an unhappy coincidence... but I didn't believe in coincidences.

What urban legend were they talking about? It could have been a million things. Perhaps Jake had a wart and wanted to rub a toad on it so it would go away. Maybe he wanted to call Bloody Mary in a mirror three times. Those two cops could've been talking about anything. That was what I got for eavesdropping.

After their little exchange, Jake went upstairs, and Blake came back into the kitchen with us girls to finish his meal.

"Blake, did you know John Roy too?" Aunt Astrid asked.

"No, ma'am, I didn't. I'm not on the softball team. I'm more of a chess player." His face was as friendly as that of a stone gargoyle.

"We were going to play Scrabble tonight," Aunt Astrid said. "You are more than welcome to join us."

For a second, I froze, waiting for Bea or Aunt Astrid to tell Blake I had eaten the beans in my taco salad. Thankfully, they spared me the humiliation.

"I'd like to, but I can't. I have some things I need to do before I call it a night." He stood up, wiping his mouth with a paper napkin.

"Well, at least take a slice of pie home for dessert." Aunt Astrid cut him a thick slice. It was almost half the pie. There went the slice I'd planned to take home myself to have for breakfast.

"I'm going to go check on Jake." Bea headed toward the stairs. "Will we see you tomorrow for breakfast, Blake?"

"Yes. It's my turn to drive, so I'll be here at the regular time."

Bea smiled and waved good-bye then went to tend to her husband.

I stepped on the wooden step stool Bea kept in the corner of the kitchen and pulled a Tupperware box down, handing it to my aunt. She gently scooped the pie into the container, snapped it shut, and handed it to Blake with a smile.

"How is the new puppy?" she asked, making me do a double take.

"You have a dog?" I asked, surprised.

"Yes." He looked more at Aunt Astrid than me. "I picked him up from that animal shelter you visit so often."

"Old Murray's place?" I couldn't help but smile. Old Murray had often taken in Treacle after he'd been out tomcatting around for a couple of nights. He'd given Treacle a nice brushing before I'd come to pick him up. He took very good care of all his animals, which was important to me.

"Yes." Blake finally looked at me. "He's not really a puppy, though. Mr. Murray had told me he was hoping someone would rescue the canine soon, and when I heard that..." He looked back at Aunt Astrid. "I had to take him home with me."

"You are a good man, Detective. What did you name him?" my aunt asked, smiling.

"I was told his name was Frank. I thought it fit."

"What kind of dog is he?" I asked.

"I wasn't really looking for a specific breed," Blake snapped back.

"No, I didn't think you were. I just wondered if he was—"

"I mean if I wanted a purebred, I would have gotten one."

"Well, yeah, of course, but—"

"It has been proven over and over that mutts often display higher levels of intelligence than even the most highly trained German shepherd or Doberman."

"I've heard that too," Aunt Astrid piped up. That comment earned her a glare from me.

"Okay, well, that was all..." Before I could even finish the sentence, Blake had his king-size slice of pie in his hands and was heading toward the front door.

"I really have to get going. Please tell Jake I'll swing by Mrs. Roy's house tonight and check on her. Thanks again for the pie." And out the door he went.

I looked at my aunt. She just smiled at me and began cleaning up the kitchen.

"Okay, you were here," I said. "You saw how he acted toward me. What is that guy's problem?"

"I'm really not sure what you're talking about, Cath. Detective Samberg is a very intense man. He's single. He's used to things being a certain way. His line of work must be stressful and demanding, so that's how he copes."

"Why are you sticking up for him?" I asked while running water in the sink so I could help rinse off the dirty dishes. I handed each one to my aunt, who then loaded them into the dishwasher. "He's never nice to me."

"Oh, you're exaggerating."

"You heard him just now." I shook my head in defeat. "You can't ask that guy a simple question without getting some kind of condescending dissertation as a reply."

My aunt chuckled. Just then, Bea appeared.

"How's the big guy doing?" I asked.

"He's all right. Tired. That kind of news makes the body feel like it just ran a marathon it hadn't trained for. He's washing up, and I told him to get into bed, put on some old movie, and leave the tube on until he falls asleep. His mind needs to zone out for a little while."

She picked up the bowl my salad had been in and brought it to me at the sink. "Thanks for helping."

I furrowed my eyebrows. "Of course. You look like you've got something else on your mind."

Bea was so much more to me than my cousin. She was my best friend, and as scary as it might be, she knew more about my past than anyone else. I trusted her with it. I was able to confide in her, knowing that if I asked her to keep something under her hat, no other soul would ever pull that secret from her. And of course, the feeling was mutual.

So when I saw her face with a few extra worry wrinkles around the eyes, I had to ask.

"I'm wondering why this is bothering Jake so much." She climbed up on one of the stools at her island and sat down. "He's usually pretty good at leaving the office *at* the office, you know. But this… this is different. There's a bee in his bonnet."

"Well, you take care of him, and we'll get out of your hair," Aunt Astrid said, wiping her hands on a towel then handing it to me to do the same. She walked over to the corner of the room and scooped up the heavy white cat. Marshmallow purred her approval and nuzzled my aunt's chin.

"Call me if you need me," I said to Bea.

"Even if I don't, I might call you anyways." She leaned in and gave me a peck on the cheek. Then she hugged her mom, scratched Marshmallow's head, and we left the house.

The sun set earlier at this time of year, and the temperature had dropped a good ten degrees since we'd arrived at Bea's house around five o'clock that evening. My long-sleeve blouse was barely enough material to keep out the chill.

Someone on the block had their fireplace burning. The smell of the smoldering wood brought back memories of Halloweens past and piles of fall leaves that I had jumped in over the years.

"The air smells good," I said, walking my aunt to her house. I looked at her when she didn't reply. "What's on your mind?"

Still, my aunt said nothing. She just looked ahead as we walked across the street.

"She sees something," Marshmallow said. *"Something is coming."*

"Is it bad or good?" I asked.

"I don't know. But it's weaving in and out of the dimensions. She's looking but can't seem to get a lock on it."

"Does it have anything to do with Jake? Or Mr. Roy?"

"It's too early to tell."

"What was that you were saying, Cath?" Aunt Astrid finally asked.

"Oh, I was just babbling about how much I like fall. What were you looking at?"

"I'm not sure yet, honey. It might be nothing, but then again..."

Standing at the edge of my aunt's porch, I waited

in the warm yellow glow of her porch light as she let herself and Marshmallow inside.

"See you at the café tomorrow," she said waving. She would shut the door then stand in the window and watch me cross the street again, and let myself into my own home. It was a ritual, ensuring everyone made it home safely.

Once my key had flipped the lock and I switched the foyer light on, I waved back to her, stepped inside, and locked the door behind me.

I went and turned on a couple of lights, making sure everything looked as though it was where it should be. Then I heard scratching at my kitchen window.

"I wonder who that is?" I asked out loud.

Pulling the curtain aside, I saw those jade-green eyes I had grown to love. Flipping the latch, I slid the window and the screen up, and in came Treacle.

"It's getting cold out there," I said to him.

"Yes, it is. I'm hungry."

"Okay, how about some yummy salmon and bacon Friskies?"

"Yes, yes, yes." He purred, rubbing his head back and forth against my leg.

After Treacle had filled his belly and begun his grooming process, we both curled up in my bed to watch a black-and-white movie about a detective, a double-cross, and a damsel in distress.

"So, what's new in the world?" I asked Treacle. *"Anything exciting going on out there?"*

Treacle looked at me with contented, sleepy eyes, his tail gently waving as if he didn't have a care in the world. *"Actually, no,"* he replied. *"And that in itself is a little weird."*

"How do you mean?"

"Well, it might be nothing, but I saw the curler lady out raking leaves."

"You mean Mrs. Greene?"

Mrs. Greene got her newspaper every morning while she still had curlers in her hair, and not the trendy new soft kind that someone could practically sleep in. We were talking the old-fashioned, plastic, bristly kind that poked your head.

"Yeah, she was out raking her leaves," Treacle said. *"I followed a field mouse into her wood pile, and while I was waiting it out, I watched her. It was like she kept raking the same spot over and over again. Then the next day, I happened to be at the same wood pile, and it was like she hadn't moved from the day before."*

"That is a little weird," I said. *"But Mrs. Greene is a little weird, so I don't know if that is a good example."*

"True."

"It might just be the season."

"Yeah, maybe that's it." Treacle didn't sound convinced.

I fell asleep with the television on and woke up an hour later to some infomercial about a new way to chop onions. Grabbing the remote, I flipped off the set. Treacle was still in bed next to me, and when I stirred, his purring started as if a switch had been flipped somewhere on his body.

I reached down and scratched his ears. *"Good night, Treacle."*

"Good night, Cath."

We both slept soundly and didn't wake up until the sun was on the horizon. After I got up, I let Treacle outside, and off he went in the direction of heaven only knew what. I got dressed in my denim finery and a soft, warm sweater and headed toward the center of town where the Brew-Ha-Ha Café was located.

It only took me about fifteen minutes to get there at a casual stroll. And my odometer was always set to casual stroll. But as I walked, I felt something different in the air, as though nothing was moving but me. There was no breeze. No cars were going down the street, and none of my neighbors were out and about performing their own morning rituals of opening garage doors or picking up newspapers.

I tried to remember if I had *ever* seen that little activity at that time of day. I couldn't put my finger on it, but there was definitely *something* in the air that made me feel as though something was wrong.

I knew that sounded like nonsense.

But just wait. It gets better.

Black-Eyed Kids

❧

That day was the first of October. The
Brew-Ha-Ha Café was decorated for
Halloween on the first of October every
year it had been open. I expected to see Bea and
Aunt Astrid already busy at work in the windows,
hanging black streamers with elegant orange-and-
yellow baubles on the ends, or arranging the spooky
little glass town with its graveyard and haunted
mansion.

Instead, I saw a dark café. Even Kevin, our baker,
who was always on time if not early, was just pulling
in as I unlocked the front door.

"Yikes!" he called to me, waving from his car
window. "Don't know what happened there. I over-
slept or something."

"No worries." I waved back. "Looks like you aren't the only one. I'll get the back door for you." I smiled at him as I stepped inside the front door. Making my way through the café, I hurried to the kitchen, flipped on the two ovens to get them warmed up, and unlocked the back entrance for Kevin.

He was a pleasant guy who really knew his way around a kitchen. Even if he showed up at noon and insisted on wearing a tiara and heels as he worked, it would be near impossible to meet someone who was as gifted in the baking department as he was.

I went back up to the front of the shop and began pulling out the Halloween decorations that were stored in the short hallway leading to our cellar, which we referred to as our secret bunker. There were seven boxes in total. As the coffee began to brew and the ovens began to give off a warm, wonderful smell of bread and pie, I started decorating and wondered where the rest of my family was.

Finally, at about ten minutes to seven, the time we opened, Bea came rushing in.

"My gosh!" she said. "I'm so sorry I'm late! Mom is right behind me!"

"Yeah, right? What the heck, girl?" I teased. "I

think you were late once about ten years ago. This kind of insubordination just won't be tolerated. You can bet it's going in your permanent file."

"No, not that!"

We both giggled.

"How's Jake feeling?" I asked while filling the sugar bowls with packets of sugar and placing cute pumpkin and ghost figurines on the tables.

"I want to tell you, but I'm waiting for Mom. You guys are not going to believe what happened this morning." She shook her head. "When Blake came by, I thought he and Jake would just head off to work together with Jake feeling more like himself. But I saw there was something wrong... Well, just wait for Mom. I don't want to have to repeat the whole thing twice."

I nodded and patted her on the back. "Sure."

I looked at the door, hoping Aunt Astrid was just a few steps away so Bea could let me in on her big to-do. I'd never had much patience. But my aunt wasn't in view yet, so I had no choice but to wait.

By the time Aunt Astrid showed up, the place was completely decorated. The morning crowd of coffee drinkers and tea sippers had already filled the dining area and formed a line that kept the front door propped open.

Of course we had a busier-than-normal morning. Any other morning, we would have had a steady stream of customers that would have died down around ten o'clock, when everyone was expected at their jobs. But not that day, not when Bea had some juicy bit of excitement to share. Nope. That was when the entire population of Wonder Falls plus a couple of neighboring cities decided they wanted coffee from the Brew-Ha-Ha. It was one o'clock in the afternoon before the place calmed down.

"And so, why were you late, young lady?" I asked my aunt with my hands on my hips, tapping my foot.

Aunt Astrid rolled her eyes. She explained that something, she didn't know what, was urging her to reinforce the protection spell on all three of our houses.

"I don't know if I had a dream or a vision in my sleep, but I woke up feeling like there was a slow leak in a tire on my car. Except I don't have a car." Bea and I looked at each other. "So, I stepped outside myself for just a moment and..."

"Mom! You know you aren't supposed to do any astral projection without someone there with you to guide you back if you get lost. Isn't that what you've told Cath and I since we were kids?"

Bea was not joking. If Aunt Astrid projected her

consciousness to a dimension or realm outside her physical body, it could have left room for any transient spirit to declare squatter's rights inside of her. There were certain steps to take that ensured that didn't happen, and probably the most important was to never do it alone.

"I know. I should practice what I preach. But as you can see, I made it back just fine. And in the few seconds I was out, I saw what looked like a little spiritual wear and tear on the protection spells around our homes."

Bea folded her arms over her chest and pursed her lips together, letting her mother know she was more than a little disappointed in her reckless behavior.

Aunt Astrid reached out her hand and tenderly rubbed her daughter's arm. "But as I inspected the damage a bit closer, it no longer looked like old-fashioned wear and tear. It looked like something had been trying to chew its way in."

"What?" I asked, loud enough that all the patrons in the café looked up at me. "Sorry, folks." I made a motion that mimicked I was zipping and locking my mouth closed.

"A parasite?" Bea asked.

Aunt Astrid nodded. "A real nasty one too."

Bea stood at her usual spot behind the counter, close to the register. I was standing in front of the counter, and my aunt was to my left.

"I think you guys better sit down," Bea said, looking out the glass door to the street. "I have to tell you what Blake told Jake and I this morning over breakfast. I'm afraid we might have more to worry about than that."

My aunt and I looked at each other then quickly took seats at the counter. We all looked around to see if any patrons needed our immediate assistance and decided whatever refill or warm-up they required could wait.

"When Blake left our house yesterday, he said he was going to go and check up on Mrs. Roy and see if she was able to answer some questions."

According to Bea, Blake had said he'd begun to feel a weird sense of being watched as he maneuvered his way through the fancy Prestwick neighborhood. But since he'd been in a moving vehicle and dealt with the facts and nothing but the facts, he'd shaken it off. He was not like Jake, who had accepted some exposure to the paranormal world just by being married to Bea. But even Jake was on a strictly need-to-know basis. Blake would never consider that something insidious could be lurking around the next dimensional corner, ready to pounce.

Blake said he kept getting turned around in the dark, trying to follow the winding roads yet ending up back at the same place, feeling as though he had jogged right when he'd meant to jog left, unsure of how he'd managed to drive around in a circle.

Finally, at a speed of about five miles an hour, he had made it to the Roy household. Mrs. Roy had been on the phone when he rang her doorbell. She'd smiled weakly but looked sad, and it was obvious to Blake that she had recently composed herself.

At hearing that, I felt a pang in my own heart for Mrs. Roy. I didn't know her, but I understood her. It was bad enough having lost a loved one to old age when the family was aware the end was coming. Even if a loved one passed from a disease, the family had a little time, even if it was short, to try and adjust. But having someone ripped away from you... that had to be the worst feeling—helplessness. I swallowed hard and tried to focus on what Bea was saying.

After Mrs. Roy let Blake in, she cried some more into the phone as she talked to her mother. She wore a T-shirt and sweatpants, and had no makeup on.

Her eyes were puffy, and the house smelled strongly of coffee.

After a few minutes, she hung up the phone and offered Blake a seat in her kitchen. True to his nature, he told Mrs. Roy he was sorry to bother her but needed a few questions answered, then he would leave her to tend to her business.

Lisa Roy outlined the day as if it were nothing special. John had been fine until she'd left for the store in the early evening.

"I had forgotten eggs, or milk, or butter, or something." She paused for a second, trying to remember why she had gone to the store, then shook her head. "I can't remember."

Blake gently urged her to continue.

"So, when I got home and stepped into the house, John came flying from the kitchen, dashing toward the front door as if he were going to run outside. But when he saw me there, he stopped dead in his tracks and looked at me."

Blake said Lisa had looked directly into his eyes as she'd spoken. There was no shiftiness or agitation in her facial expression or voice. He was convinced she was telling him the truth.

"When I looked at him," she continued, "I saw a man who was terrified out of his mind. John was all pale. His eyes were wide, and he was sweating terribly."

Lisa told Blake that John had kept repeating, "They said they needed to use the phone." He'd said it over and over as he searched the house.

"Who?" Lisa asked while she took off her jacket and hung her purse on the peg across from the door. "Who needed to use the phone?"

"The two kids," John said. "The two kids I let in the house. They just said they needed to use the phone."

Lisa suddenly became very afraid. For some crazy reason, John had let two people in the house to use the phone. He was a trial attorney who did work with the public defender's office. He was no stranger to the seedier elements of life, and he knew better than to let strangers into the house.

Blake asked her if she had seen the people John had let in and if she could give him a description, but she shook her head. Lisa insisted she never saw the people or kids John had claimed he let in the house. She said John had taken both of her hands in his, and she had felt them trembling.

"Their eyes. Their eyes were completely black," John had said.

Both Aunt Astrid and I sat back when we heard that, as if we had both been given a jolt of electricity.

"Contact lenses." Lisa had insisted as she tried to calm her husband down. She looked at Blake, shaking her head and repeating how she knew it all sounded crazy and that it probably didn't even mean anything. If there were any people in the house and they did have black eyes, Lisa was convinced they were teenagers or young adults getting into the Halloween spirit or rebelling against their parents and society at large by being creepy.

Blake asked her where John had said the kids went, but Lisa gave him a very strange answer. She said John didn't know. According to John, they'd shown up at the door. He'd let them in. They scared the hell out of him, and just as he was about to run out of the house, Lisa had come home and the kids were gone. Vanished.

Of course, Blake asked if she had searched the house, and she said she had. She grabbed a carving knife from the cutlery block in the kitchen, and with her husband, John, begging her to just leave with him, she searched every room. They went down into the basement and checked every corner, even places they both knew no human could fit. They even checked the attic that could only be accessed by a ladder that pulled down from the ceiling and made enough noise to wake the dead in the cemetery ten miles away.

Lisa continued, saying John had insisted there were two pale-faced children who came to the door and asked to use the phone. He said he had let them in even though something inside him had screamed at him to slam the door shut. And after the kids were in the house and the door was shut behind them, they had looked at John with black, bottom-less eyes.

"Oh dear," Aunt Astrid said. "That is very weird."

Bea nodded and covered her heart with her left hand. She felt a great deal of sadness and confusion about the situation, but not just from Jake. A good deal of Lisa's emotional trauma had rubbed off on Blake. When he'd come over to Bea's house that morning, he had a negative residue on him and didn't even know it.

"But it gets worse," Bea said.

Lisa had gone on to say that John had been acting strangely the whole night. Even after they'd checked the whole house, he couldn't seem to wind down. He'd paced as if he were a caged tiger and kept mumbling to himself, acting like someone who was in a huge hurry to leave but couldn't find his keys. In bed, he'd tossed and turned the entire night, insisting all the lights in the lower part of the house stayed on just in case they had to get down the stairs quickly. More than once when his eyelids had gotten too heavy to fight, he'd dozed for a couple minutes then sat bolt upright, looking around frantically and whimpering as though he were a child who had woken up to find his nightlight had gone out.

Finally, after neither of them had slept much, the sun began to lighten the sky. John got out of bed and began walking the floors. Lisa couldn't sleep with him in that kind of state, so she got up and made coffee. She suggested they both take a personal day and told John to relax and take a hot shower. She told him to stay in his pajamas and forget what had happened the night before.

"He wouldn't relax," Lisa said. She insisted he had tried, but he kept looking over his shoulder as if someone were sneaking up on him. He kept dropping things, bumping into things, and tripping over his own feet. It was as though his whole equilibrium had been thrown off.

At three o'clock in the morning, he had gone upstairs without saying a word to Lisa. The next thing she knew, she heard a huge crash and ran upstairs to find that the window to the master bedroom had been broken out. There was blood on the broken shards of glass that were still in the window frame.

It hadn't crossed her mind that John had jumped out. She just wondered what the heck had happened to the window? Who had thrown something through the window? Why was there blood? But as she called for John, she realized the house had become eerily quiet.

Hearing that sent a shiver up my spine as I recalled how quiet it had been that morning on my way to the café.

Stepping to the edge of the window, Lisa had peered out and seen John's body lying face down with shards of glass and broken pieces of wood from the frame all around him.

She ran downstairs, tore open the front door, pulled her cell phone from her pocket, and dialed 9-1-1.

The Red-Eye

B lake said her eyes welled up with tears
again as she wrapped up her story.

"I just kept asking John to hold on and
asking why," Lisa had said. "Why would he do this
to himself? Why would he leave me all alone? I held
his hand and could feel bones rolling around inside,
broken and ripped from their muscles. I told him not
to move. I don't know if he heard me or not. His
eyes were barely open. So much blood was coming
out of his ears."

"So what did Samberg think of all this?" I asked
Bea. I couldn't help but think a guy so grounded in
reality would have felt as though she were yanking
his chain.

Bea shrugged. "Blake said he didn't know what to

think about Lisa's story. But he did say that if there were some local kids around playing tricks on the more seasoned citizens of Wonder Falls, and this was the result... well, I don't have to tell you how he'd plan on handling it. He doesn't play."

"No, he doesn't," I concurred. I thought back to the one time I had seen Blake interrogate a suspect. It was my good friend Min. Even though Blake had been wrong to think Min had anything to do with the crime, he'd certainly known how to interrogate. Heaven help the guy or guys who Blake had to interrogate for this prank.

"So, are we talking about what I think we're talking about?" Aunt Astrid asked, standing up and shuffling behind the counter to grab the full pot of coffee. "This sounds like black-eyed children." She went around to the tables, making a little small talk as she refilled coffee cups and picked up empty dishes.

I looked at Bea with wide eyes. "I thought black-eyed children were an urban legend—Internet hoaxes like Slender Man and *The Grudge* type of stories."

"I don't know," Bea said, "but remember, I had to blow this off like it was a whole lot of hoo-ha. I couldn't tell Blake that back before the trials in

1692, women in the craft could often change their eye color to blue, green, brown, and sometimes black just as easily as they could change their clothes. I couldn't let on that in other instances, jet-black eyes indicated something was possessed by a demon."

"Or demons," Aunt Astrid added.

"But that's if we believe this was a real occurrence and not what Samberg says it is," I said. "A couple of kids playing games and freaking people out just for the fun of it. What do we do?"

Aunt Astrid put the coffee pot back on the burner and turned to face Bea and me. "I'll tell you what we need to do. We need to do some research and find out if anywhere in history, these kinds of things have been seen before. Cath, bring your laptop to my house and check on the Internet to see if you notice any similarities in any of the stories online or if you think they're mostly fiction. Bea, you can help me look through the library and see if we can find any references to children with black eyes. That is where I suggest we start." Aunt Astrid pushed her wild, flowing locks back behind her shoulder and straightened her back.

"So meet at your house. Will there be food there?" I asked.

"Maybe we should order some Chinese food?" Bea suggested.

"Count me in." I grabbed a rag and got to work, cleaning up the empty tables and washing the dishes.

I was surprised the rest of the afternoon went by smoothly and without any crisis or incident. Plenty of our regular customers came in, including my friend Min and his sweetheart Amalia.

"Hey, Cath!" She waved excitedly as she walked in. "I gotta ask you a favor."

"Okay." I looked her up and down suspiciously. "Step into my office." We took a couple of steps away from the counter as Min gave me a happy wave and talked with Bea. "What can I do for you?"

"Min mentioned to me that you were a really fantastic artist," she said.

I shook my head, a little surprised. I had loved to draw in high school, and I wasn't bad at it, but I'd never thought I was fantastic. I kept most of my artistic endeavors to myself. Only Treacle knew that I kept a sketchpad under my bed, and that was only because he was one of my favorite subjects.

"I've been known to dabble. Why?"

She looked around at Min then back at me, putting her hand up as if whispering a secret.

"Min's birthday is coming up."

"Holy moly! You're right. I completely forgot. Thanks for reminding me."

"Hey, no biggie," she said. "But what I wanted to ask you was if you thought you could draw a picture for Min's birthday. I'll pay you, of course. And I'll take care of putting it in a frame. But I think it would be an awesome gift to give him. We can even make it from both of us."

"Well, I think I could if you give me a picture to draw from. And I'd never take any money from you for it. That is out of the question."

"I've got a picture already. I was hoping you'd say yes." She giggled joyfully as she dug in her purse, which was the size of a small suitcase. She pulled out an envelope to hand to me, and she was practically bouncing with excitement. I tucked it into my back pocket just as Min was sauntering over, holding two to-go cups of Bea's fabulous tea with lavender-infused honey.

"What are you two talking about?" he asked, leaning in to give me a peck on the cheek.

"Nothing," Amalia said. "Just plotting world domination one coffee shop at a time. You want in?"

"Is that all?" Min asked.

"That and where to get some really tasty barbeque ribs."

I couldn't help but laugh. Amalia came up with the oddest things to say, but she was the only person I knew who could get away with saying them and sound totally sane.

"What are you guys doing tonight?" I asked, waiting to hear the details of some horribly romantic plan that included champagne and rose petals and violins.

"I've actually got to catch a red-eye to New York tonight," Min said. "I have a meeting with some board members for I can't even remember what. So this tea is about it, then I'll be on my way."

"I've got a double shift at the nursing home, so I'm going to work and then recuperate for another two days."

"It's tough having to work for a living, isn't it?" I asked.

"Yeah, if only we knew someone who could pay all our bills and buy all our groceries for us all the time," Amalia said with such a hysterically funny serious face that I thought I was going to bust a gut.

"They should pay just to be our friends," I added.

"Right?" She looked up at Min and started to laugh.

"I think I might start paying to keep you two away from each other," he said. "Amalia, you're a bad influence. Or wait, is it Cath who's the bad influence? Either way, you two together are too much."

I laughed and slipped behind the counter. I grabbed two homemade biscotti dipped in caramel and chocolate, tossed them into one of our festive orange-and-purple Halloween Brew-Ha-Ha carry-out bags, and handed them to Amalia.

"On the house. And Amalia, stop in after you've recovered from your double shift. We can talk some more."

"I'll do that."

She and Min waved good-bye and left the café. Just a short while later, we were all locking the place up and arranging to meet at Aunt Astrid's house for some research and Chinese food.

I really didn't expect for things to take the turn they did.

The Happy Family

❧

When I got home, I went to my bedroom and pulled out my sketchbook and pencils. The pages mostly contained detailed images of Treacle. I drew them as lifelike as I could.

There were also a couple of drawings of the Brew-Ha-Ha immediately after the fire. I had gone back in the early morning after the investigation of the mysterious fire to scribble a few sketches.

I'd also drawn a caricature of Darla as a zombie that felt extremely satisfying to put on paper. I'd made sure every boil, blister, and patch of decay was as realistic as possible. The picture made me smile every time I saw it.

After tossing the book and pencils on my bed, I pulled the envelope out of my pocket and threw it on top of them. I'd start drawing later. I grabbed my laptop and headed back out, happy that I had some research and Chinese food to tend to.

As I walked down the sidewalk and crossed the street, I noticed that the tension I had felt in the air that morning was gone. I saw people driving, raking leaves, and jogging. My little part of Wonder Falls seemed back to normal, at least. Who knew what was going on just one block over? The world could have dropped off over there, and I would never know it.

After I let myself into Aunt Astrid's house, I inhaled deeply, smelling the wonderful aroma of egg rolls and my favorite, beef and peppers.

"Hey, we got you some tofu and sprouts," Bea shouted from the kitchen. I passed by a stack of paperback novels on Aunt Astrid's coffee table as I walked through the living room. She had a frighteningly complete collection of Jackie Collins novels, her guilty pleasure.

"I do hope you're kidding," I said as I stepped into the kitchen. Unlike Bea's very modern home, Aunt Astrid had a flair for the traditional. The walls of her kitchen were painted an olive green. Everyone gathered around a thick oak table that had a bench on one side and mismatched chairs on the other. Her living room was boho-chic to match her peace-and-love attitude. And every flat surface was covered with at least one stack of books.

I cleared myself a small square of wood on the bench at the table, sat down, and propped my computer up on a stack of books so I could eat while I did my research.

"Bea, don't tease your cousin so much. It isn't her fault she can eat anything she wants and not gain a pound." Aunt Astrid placed my container of pepper steak, rice, and three egg rolls in front of me.

I looked over the books at Bea, who was crossing her eyes at me.

"Oh, what did you get?" I asked her, more concerned with food at the moment than black-eyed tweens or anything that might be chewing at our psychically implemented security system.

"The Happy Family. Mixed veggies in a lobster sauce, no MSG."

My aunt had what she always had—an extra-large container of shrimp fried rice that she would stretch out for three days.

We began to eat, and the food was delicious. But as the evening went on and we read more and more stories about black-eyed kids, we started to realize that what Lisa Roy had told Detective Samberg might have been more sinister than we'd first imagined.

I knew I couldn't always believe what I read on the Internet. But true or not, the stories were still pretty compelling.

One woman claimed a black-eyed kid robbed her of her casino winnings in Florida. A dude in New Mexico claimed he'd seen an army of them flood off a space ship. My personal favorite was a lady in Portland, Oregon who claimed to have been impregnated by a black-eyed man and said she had black-eyed twins as a result. Of course, when asked to produce the little bundles of joy, she revealed they were with their father on the planet Seti-Alpha Five.

"I'm not really finding anything that doesn't sound like memoirs of a crackpot." I shut my laptop and took another bite of egg roll.

"Yeah. I can't say I'm finding anything too substantial here either," Bea said, closing a big green book with worn and weathered yellow pages.

Aunt Astrid stood up and stretched. "We just

don't have enough to go on." She stifled a yawn. "If only we could have talked to John before he..."

"Took his big leap," I said.

"Cath, have a little compassion," Bea said. "We don't know if these beings had something to do with his suicide or if he was really torn up on the inside due to some other influence."

"I wasn't trying to be funny, but it is what the guy did. And I for one think that maybe there was more to the story than we or even Samberg were told."

"Like what?" Bea asked.

"I don't know. Did the guy ever do any drugs? Was he in a place where there were toxic fumes? Had he hit his head recently? Was there a history of crazy in his family? I'm not saying Lisa Roy wasn't telling the truth. I'm just saying, with the only connection to these kids being six feet underground, it's anyone's guess as to what they really are, if they are real at all."

Both Bea and my aunt looked at me thoughtfully.

"Or I could be wrong." I shrugged.

We all sat quietly for a second. Bea twisted a couple of strands of her beautiful red hair, and Aunt Astrid tried to peer around a corner in a dimension only she could see. I couldn't resist another bite of pepper steak just as I heard a frantic knocking at the door.

Before any of us could move, the door opened. My assumptions about these black-eyed kids immediately changed. We realized we were all in trouble.

Exploding Head Syndrome

❧

"**O**h, my God!" Bea cried. "Jake! What's the matter?"

Jake stumbled inside, fell to his knees, and nearly passed out on the floor with his feet still partially on the porch.

I jumped up and ran out front, looking around for anyone or anything that might have been trying to make a getaway, but the street was deserted. It had that same eerie quiet, as if everything was holding its breath. Without anyone to chase or call after, I darted back inside the house. We pulled Jake's size-fourteen feet inside so we could shut the door tightly.

Bea immediately began to work on him. She ran her hands up and down his arms and legs. Making circles over his chest, she closed her eyes and mumbled a request for help from all of nature and the life force around us.

"What do you see, Bea?" Aunt Astrid asked nervously.

"He's been attacked. It looks to me like he made someone or something very mad. There are scratches on the walls of his mind. His heart has been bruised. Whatever did this wanted to hurt him, but from what I can tell, Jake was able to fight it off."

"Is he dying?" I asked, my eyes filling with tears as I looked down at the big, strong ox whom I loved as a brother lying helpless and almost unconscious on the hardwood floor.

"No," Bea snapped back. "He is not dying, but he's badly hurt. We need to get him to the spare room."

The three of us had a heck of a time trying to get Jake to his feet. He could barely stand and seemed as helpless and unsteady as a newborn colt. His legs visibly shook underneath him, and he was drenched in sweat. When we finally got him close enough to the bed, he flopped down with a *thump* onto the soft blankets, and the old bedsprings creaked out an objection at being forced to support something heavier than a cat.

Once Bea got Jake out of his shoes and removed his belt, she tucked him underneath the cover.

She turned to Aunt Astrid. "I don't want to move him."

"Of course, honey. He can stay here," Aunt Astrid reassured her. "As long as he needs to. I'll get some sage burning. The white candles and crow feathers will be gathered, too. He's safer here than anywhere else, Bea."

I told Marshmallow and Peanut Butter to stay close.

"Do either of you sense anything?" I asked them. *"Anything at all that might still be lurking around outside? Anything that might have attached itself to Jake?"*

"I don't sense anything," Peanut Butter said. *"Why? Should I? I can try a little harder and see what happens."*

I shook my head and scratched him under the chin.

"I thought I did when he first came in," Marshmallow said. *"But whatever it was let go. It's long gone by now."*

I called to Treacle in my mind. He answered me almost immediately and said there was nothing strange going on around him. I told him to be careful, and I suggested he stay either closer to home or Old Murray's shelter, just in case.

Marshmallow hopped up on the bed and curled

up by Jake's feet. Peanut Butter stretched out along the bookshelf that stood by the headboard. I patted Marshmallow behind the ears, and as I left the bedroom, I could hear the two cats purring their own vigil for Jake.

Bea came into the room with warm water, a washcloth, a raw egg, and some salt.

"Aunt Astrid is right," I said. "This is where he'll get the best care." I took Bea's hands in my own and squeezed them. "He'll be all right, and we'll find out what did this. And we'll give it such an ass—"

Bea cut me off as she usually did when I was about to cuss. But this time, she cut me off with a hug.

I hugged her back tightly. "He'll be okay, Bea. With you at his side, he'll always be okay."

She nodded. I could tell Bea was trying to hold it together. She went into the spare room, sat down next to Jake, took his hand in hers, and began to quietly chant a healing rite.

I stayed with them through the night. Jake was getting better and better by the minute, but Bea was exhausted. She believed a few more incantations would heal the damage the unknown fright had caused him. He wasn't talking yet, but he'd stopped shaking, his temperature was closer to normal, and he seemed to be sleeping the kind of deep sleep of a person who had hiked for over an hour uphill through four feet of snow. Something had attacked his mind and exhausted him trying to get in.

When it was almost daylight, I looked outside to see if anything was out of the ordinary. Nope. It all looked normal.

"Aunt Astrid," I said quietly as she began to make coffee in the kitchen. "I'm going to go to my place and change clothes. I want to just give the place a quick once-over, you know, just in case."

"Yes, honey, go ahead. I've put an extra spell over everyone, so you should be safe. But I don't have to tell you if there is any trouble, you run those legs back over here and don't stop until the door is shut behind you."

"I will. I think I'll check the café too. I'll drive if that makes you feel any better."

"It does, Cath. Thanks."

Before I left, I asked her if she had seen anything in her study of the other dimensions in front of us. She still continued to look a bit past me as though something were just beyond a curtain, but she couldn't quite make it out. Not yet.

AFTER CLEANING UP AT MY PLACE, I CLIMBED into my car and headed off in the direction of the Brew-Ha-Ha. It was still very early. Most people were probably getting ready to head to work.

I couldn't help but let my mind drift to something I had read recently.

I'd heard about a new phenomenon discovered by scientists called Exploding Head Syndrome. It wasn't nearly as gruesome as it sounded. People who suffered from the affliction often heard loud noises in their heads like gunshots, breaking glass, and doors slamming when they were dosing off or in a very light sleep. Those loud noises startled the afflicted people into alertness, and in most cases, made them run around their houses checking for fallen mirrors, broken windows, or even thwarted break-ins. But of course, they would find nothing and just chalk it up to a vivid dream they couldn't remember.

The scientists who had identified that singularity considered it an odd action of the brain.

But a witch like me knew better. Sometimes I wondered how the scientific community had come so far from its paranormal roots.

Exploding Head Syndrome was not just a trick or hiccup in the brain. It was actually a very valuable talent. Some people were good at math. Some people could paint. Some people were fantastic athletes. And some people could hear other beings entering and exiting alternate dimensions. Those loud crashes and door slams were mere echoes of some entity, usually a rude one, who had just pushed its way through to our dimension. But because the people didn't ask for identification or shout *halt, who goes there?* and chalked up the noise as a dream, the entity just passed along its merry way, causing whatever kind of havoc it wanted.

The people who had that gift didn't realize it, and therefore never developed it. Instead of visiting Grandma in the next city, they could have visited Grandpa who was in the alternate dimension two doors down.

But abilities like that would have been scary if someone didn't have a reference point. If I hadn't known about my witchy heritage before I realized I could talk to an animal telepathically, I would have had myself committed and the key thrown away. I began to wonder if John Roy had been such a person. He may have never known why he was able to hit all the green lights coming home when he was in a hurry or how he was always able to help his wife find her keys when she misplaced them.

Unfortunately, he was in a morgue and destined to be buried within the next forty-eight hours. There was no chance for Bea to get a peek at him to see if there was any paranormal residue left on him from the tragedy.

Aunt Astrid said she had felt something was floating through the dimensions, but whatever it was was moving at a glacial pace and not stirring up any trouble. However, she wasn't sure if it was a natural ripple in the time and space current, if something was just lazily drifting through the astral plains, or if something more insidious was inching its way along, hoping it wouldn't be noticed.

I couldn't help it. Worrying about Jake wasn't going to do anyone any good, so I decided I needed to keep busy. And what harm would there be if I just took a drive past the Roy residence, right? I didn't ask anyone's permission, which guaranteed no one would tell me no. But I had a feeling I was going to have to ask for forgiveness when I was all through.

Prestwick

✿

My car was a ten-year-old, teal-colored Dodge Neon. The muffler was starting to fall off, and the window on the passenger's side couldn't be rolled down without coming off the track. A couple of empty Tasty Burger sacks were crumpled up in the back seat, along with a jacket I had tossed in the back when the weather had been hot for one day before plunging back into the fifty-degree range. I wasn't the neatest person, especially compared with Bea, who had a neat streak a mile wide.

"A clean car runs better," she often insisted.

"A new car runs even better than that," I would always say back.

So I hopped in my old Neon and headed off in the

direction of the Prestwick neighborhood to see what was going on. I had no idea where the Roys lived, but I knew where Darla lived. Blake had said they were at opposite ends of the of the development, so I thought I would start at Darla's.

Crossing over to Prestwick from the normal part of town was like slipping into another dimension. There was a beautiful sign as I entered the area that was a little over four feet high, five feet thick, and seven feet wide. It was made of solid oak and had the word Prestwick carved into it in elegant, rolling script. The reason I knew it was solid oak was because if I ever encountered anyone who lived in Prestwick, they told me the story about the sign.

Some old geezer by the name of Ignace Gigot had decided he wanted the area for himself and his thoroughbred horses, so he named the place after his most prized filly, Prestwick. On his property were some huge oak trees, and during a particularly bad storm, one of the older trees was uprooted and fell. Sure, it would keep him in firewood throughout the next three winters, but he had a vision.

He chopped the wood with his own two hands. He dragged the wood to the workshop he had in his barn. He sanded, smoothed, and lovingly carved the name of his favorite horse into the giant block of tree trunk. Then, with his own bare hands, he loaded the behemoth onto his cart, which was being pulled by Prestwick herself, and carried it to the edge of the property, where it still remained.

Of course, they never mentioned that Prestwick died under the strain of pulling such a heavy load all by herself. *No, I'm just kidding. I like to add that just to mess with some of the neighborhood Prestwickans when I hear them telling that story.*

Mr. Gigot did all of the work with his own bare hands. After more and more people began to settle in and around Prestwick, the land belonging to Mr. Gigot was sold off in pieces. But residents kept the name and the history that came with it.

I pulled into Prestwick and couldn't help but notice the immediate rainbow of fall colors that arched over the streets as I drove in. Someone somewhere in their city planning committee must have made sure certain types of trees were planted in order to make one neighborhood more beautiful than another.

I came to Darla's house. It was up on a hill, of course, so that at any time day or night, she could look out any window and look down on everyone else around her. It was a beautiful home. The fact that she still got to live in it after the crimes she'd committed was a thorn in my side.

Anyway, I quickly averted my eyes as if I were in fear of turning to stone. I headed down another street in the hopes it might bring me to my destination, the Roy residence.

The roads snaked all around, and I was pretty sure I would have a hard time finding my way back to the main road. I hadn't thought to leave a mystic trail so I could find my way back. Luckily, I wasn't in any kind of danger. I was just gathering intelligence. I wasn't planning on doing battle on my own with any beasties from another dimension. Plus, even using a little of my magic would have drained my body just enough to have kept me yawning throughout the day. Staying sharp and conserving resources were more important, and who knew what Bea might need after she had stayed up the whole night tending to Jake.

But as the road began winding further and further into the neighborhood, I was startled to realize how big that part of town was. The deeper I drove, the houses became bigger and more beautiful. They made Darla's house look like a Lincoln Log set. I had to admit that gave me some level of satisfaction.

I turned onto Butternut Drive and thought I saw a street that would cut through the middle of the current subdivision I was in. As I turned onto it, I realized it wasn't a street but a driveway. The asphalt turned into beautiful, old cobblestone that looked amazing but was in bad need of repair. The shocks on my car were gone, and I felt every bump as I rolled over them.

I came to a rusted gate that blocked the drive and was joined on either side by a wrought iron fence. There were several no trespassing signs. The gate was bound shut by what looked like yards and yards of rusted chain and a padlock the size of a baseball mitt.

As I made a three-point turn that would have made any driver's ed teacher proud, I saw a sad and weather-worn For Sale sign. I wondered what was at the end of such an elaborate driveway and gate.

I made my way back down to the street and continued my search for the Roy residence. As I went back the way I had come, it was only pure chance that I came upon a house that had several cars parked in the driveway and along the street in front of the house.

Had it been me, I would have called my immediate family and closest friends for support during such a horrible tragedy. I wouldn't have wanted to be alone, and I assumed Mrs. Roy was no different. Slowly, I inched up to the mailbox and saw what I was looking for. R-O-Y. I was right.

As quietly as I could get my car to go, I passed the house completely and turned left down the nearest side street. After a quick U-turn, I was in a position to observe but not be observed. It was early, and when I shut off the car engine, I could hear the songs of the birds waking up in all the colorful trees. I looked around, hoping no one would notice me. My car stood out like a sore thumb. The cheapest ride in the Prestwick neighborhood was probably last year's BMW.

Still, I didn't want to just give up. Not yet. So I turned the heat up a bit and cracked the window, smelling the cool autumn air and the smoky smell of wood burning in a fireplace.

When I looked toward the Roys' house, I couldn't see anything out of the ordinary right off the bat. I tried to see if they had any pets in the house like a dog or a bird. But I didn't get any reply to my telepathic inquiries except from a nosy pug dog across the street that seemed to know the German Shepherd on the next block was in heat.

The window from which John Roy had jumped

was boarded up with plywood. It looked like a scab on an otherwise perfect face.

I was about to get out of the car and take a walk past the house to get a better look and try to see if there was any kind of mystical residue left when an all-too-familiar car came around the corner.

Stale Coffee

"You've got to be kidding me," I mumbled.

Blake Samberg's car was slowly pulling down the street I had just come from. Oh, my gosh. What if he had been behind me the whole time, and he knew I was snooping around?

As soon as the driver's head turned in my direction, I ducked down in my seat. This was mortifying. I held my breath as if that might help him not see me. Had I been thinking on my feet, I might have used a camouflage spell. But that required a huge output of energy, especially if I were going to conceal my car, which I would have to do. And a spell would have tipped off any thug spirits that someone was investigating. I wasn't all that keen on putting such a big target on my back so early in the game. I was just trying to collect intel. I wasn't looking for a fight.

So as I sat all scrunched down in the driver's seat, I studied the fabric of my car seats and realized they were very stained. A Jujyfruits candy box peeked out from underneath the passenger seat, and for the life of me, I couldn't remember having eaten them. I wasn't even sure I liked them.

I had a layer of dust on my console, and the leaves on the floor could have very well been there since last fall. How could I have been riding in such filth?

I leaned over and sniffed the fabric of the seat, fearing I might be accosted by some foul odor I had long since grown immune to. That was when I realized I didn't hear a car driving by. Maybe Blake was too busy looking at the Roy house to have seen me.

After I scooted up in my seat, I looked around and didn't see him. I let out a big sigh and stretched my neck to look up in the rearview mirror. Blake's car was right behind mine.

"Son of a b..."

Knock. Knock.

I looked at my passenger window and saw Blake staring right back at me. I never saw him smile, but I swear he had a devious glint in his eye that made it clear he was enjoying my embarrassment.

Without asking, he opened the door and climbed in. I really hoped my car didn't smell.

For a second, I didn't say anything as my mind raced for a plausible explanation for why I was in Prestwick a few houses down and around the corner from the Roys' house. I got lost? I was in the neighborhood?

"Funny seeing you here," Blake said.

"Yeah, well, I felt bad." It wasn't a complete lie. I did feel bad for Lisa Roy. How did a person make that phone call to her parents or to his parents and tell them what had happened? How did she put into words that the person she loved with all her heart was in such a dark, lonely place that he took his own life? And worse than that, how did she admit she hadn't seen it coming?

There wasn't a person alive who wouldn't somehow find a way to blame herself for this kind of tragedy.

Lisa Roy would be permanently crippled from then on, and no doctor, not even Bea, would be able to fix it. That kind of injury never healed.

I felt tears sting my eyes, and as I looked at Blake, my cheeks turned red. I rolled my eyes as if to say I knew my excuse sounded corny, but for a second, I saw compassion in his eyes.

Clearing my throat, I looked back at the Roy house. "So, what are you doing here? Follow-up questions?" I asked, mentally pulling myself together.

Blake looked at the house through the windshield for a moment. "Sort of. I had a gut feeling that I should stop by and just observe." He looked back at me. "I didn't think I'd have a partner to pass the time."

Okay, yes, I felt a little jitter in my stomach when he said that, and it was impossible to stop the corners of my lips from curling up at the edges.

To keep it light, I told Blake that Jake was a bit under the weather, careful not to tell him that his partner had fallen into the house after nearly having his head torn apart from the inside out.

He looked worried. "Maybe I should check up on him. I'll follow you to your aunt's house."

"Oh, no." I said, waving my hands in front of me. "It was probably something he ate. My taco salad or something." I chuckled nervously. "Bea will take good care of him."

"Yeah, well, all the same, I think—"

Before Blake could finish his sentence, a strange

truck pulled into the Roy driveway. It was an old, rusty blue pickup that belonged in the neighborhood about as much as my Dodge Neon. And when the man hopped out of the cab, he didn't act as if he were a concerned member of the family. He began marching toward the front door as if he were heading off to war.

But before he could make it to the middle of the driveway, the front door opened. An older man in his late fifties, wearing a T-shirt and sweatpants, stood there holding a shotgun. He didn't aim it or even cock it, but he just stood there.

"Oh my gosh," I whispered.

Blake and I sat there frozen just like the man in the driveway had frozen.

"I just want to talk to Lisa!" the man shouted. His blond hair was messy, and he was wearing a black T-shirt and blue jeans.

"She's got nothing to say to you!" the older man shouted back. "Now you just get in your car and get out of here!"

The blond man hesitated for a moment. I saw out of the corner of my eye that Blake was slowly reaching for the door handle with one hand and his sidearm with the other.

Thankfully, the man in the driveway thought

better of whatever it was he'd been planning. He took two steps backward then turned and got back into his truck. With a loud rev of his engine and squealing of his tires, the man peeled out of the Roys' driveway and headed in our direction.

Both Blake and I immediately ducked down in our seats, our faces nearly colliding as we hovered over the gearshift between the seats.

I held my breath, sure I smelled like stale coffee. I looked at Blake, who at first was looking over my head and out the window. His eyes were a really pretty brown that looked like carved wood. Not hard but... deep. But when they met mine, I quickly looked away as though I were a spazzy teenager. *Smooth, Cath. Real smooth.*

Finally, those few seconds, which seemed more like ten uncomfortable minutes, passed by along with the noisy truck, and Blake and I both sat up.

"Well, what the heck was that all about?" I asked. I got no answer.

Blake pulled his notebook from his pocket and began to scribble some things down.

"What are you writing?"

Still no reply.

"Let me guess. Official police business, ma'am.

Nothing to see here," I said in as deep and as serious a voice as I could muster.

Surprisingly, Blake smirked. "Make and model of the car, license plate number, and description of the driver." His voice had dropped a level lower. I guess that was his serious detective voice.

I nodded. Looking out the front windshield, I saw the front door of the Roy home was again closed tight. The entire street was quiet once more.

"I'm going to run this through the criminal database and see if we have any information on our truck-driving friend." Blake folded his notebook up and tucked it back into his inside jacket pocket. "Perhaps Mrs. Roy left out a few details."

I didn't say anything as Blake climbed out of my car. But I wondered what he would have thought of me if I'd told him the truth about my life. People kept secrets for all kinds of reasons, and not all of them were sinister. Sometimes a lie by omission was just easier.

Before shutting the door, he leaned back inside. "Tell Jake I'll call him and fill him in on what I find." Without waiting for a response, he slammed the door shut and got into his own car. Turning over the engine, he slowly and quietly drove away in the same direction the truck had gone.

"Okay, Mr. Bossy Britches," I mumbled. I went in the opposite direction, heading back the way I came, and thankfully I only got turned around one time on the way out of Prestwick. It seemed as if it were a lot easier to get out of that neighborhood than it was to get in.

What the Cat Dragged In

I swung by the Brew-Ha-Ha. Kevin was already there, and everything looked normal, so I quickly made my way back to Aunt Astrid's house.

When I stepped in the door, I smelled strong black coffee and heard Bea and her mom chatting away in the kitchen. Before I could ask what they were talking about, I heard Jake's voice. He sounded tired but otherwise like himself.

I smiled at them as I walked into the kitchen. "Boy, you sure are a drama queen," I teased. Jake was sitting on the davenport sofa in front of the sliding glass door that led to the backyard. I walked over to him and leaned in to ruffle his hair, which was already a mess. His eyes looked a little dark underneath, but they twinkled, and his smile was genuine.

Both Marshmallow and Peanut Butter were perched on each armrest as if they were furry guardians of the temple.

"Yeah?" Jake asked. "Bea told me you were at home making homemade chicken soup, so I thought I better get my butt out of bed quick."

I clicked my tongue and put my hands on my hips, looking Jake up and down. "Really? You're obviously not that sick."

Jake laughed and rubbed his head.

I went to the counter and poured myself a cup of coffee while Aunt Astrid cut me a slice of thick white bread she had baked herself. I hadn't realized how hungry I was, and that made me remember someone else who might have been hungry too.

"Treacle!" I shouted in my head. No sooner had I called to him than I heard a scratching at the door.

"Well, look who the cat dragged in," I said as the pitch-black feline snaked his way inside the house. He rubbed his sides along the door in order to remind other alley cats that this house was indeed his, no ifs, ands, or buts about it.

"Don't you ever get tired of that joke?" he asked me as if he were an annoyed teenager.

I looked into his bright-green eyes. *"No."*

He let out a terse meow as if he'd ended the conversation once and for all. With slow steps, he walked over to where Jake was sitting and sat back on his haunches. With his tail whipping back and forth, he measured the distance from the floor to the headrest. Then Treacle leapt elegantly and silently onto the chair and took his spot behind Jake's head.

With a quick show of affection, Treacle rubbed Jake's head with his own, and his purring machine was going at full speed.

There was so much good energy in the house with the entire family together that I believed Jake would find he had healed more quickly than ever before.

"So, seriously, Jake. How are you feeling?" I set my coffee cup down on a stack of books so I could remove another stack on the end of the bench at the long kitchen table.

"I feel like I drank too much but didn't taste a drop." He rubbed his eyes. "I'll be ready to go back to wo—"

"Go back to where?" Bea interrupted. "Back to bed? Yes, you'll be ready to go back to bed in just a little while."

"Blake and I are partners, and partners show up for work."

"Partners suffering from mysterious illnesses are no good to anyone," Bea added.

Jake shrugged. I thought he just wanted someone to give him permission to stay home, and Bea was happy to oblige.

"Truthfully," he started to speak. His eyes popped up from the coffee cup in his hands that he had been looking at. "I'm glad all of you are here. All of you," he said again, scratching Peanut Butter behind the ears. "There is something I need to tell you."

My eyes jumped from Bea to my aunt, back to Bea again, and then to Jake.

"Last week"—he started to rub the back of his neck as if he were a teenager getting ready to tell his dad he'd put a dent in the station wagon—"Samberg and I were wrapping up a chain of B&Es we had been investigating. Some of the file information was at Blake's place, so we stopped there. He was going to check on Frank, you know, take him for a walk, make sure he had water, and since I hadn't seen the dog, I went along with him." He put his hand down and absently rubbed Marshmallow. It was as though his hands were jittery and needed something to do, or else he might not have been able to get the story out.

"Frank is a really nice dog. A real nice dog. Yeah." Jake nodded. "Blake offered me a beer, and we were just chewing the fat about the case and talking shop when suddenly Frank started acting weird. He started to bark at the front door. And growl. It was a deep-down-from-the-gut kind of growl too, the kind that meant he wasn't playing. And he was standing at the door while he did it."

Jake shifted in the davenport, looking like a scared boy.

"Was the door open?" I asked, wondering if Frank was responding to something he had seen outside.

"No. It was shut tight and dead-bolted. And there is a screen door, and it was locked. Blake isn't the kind of guy who leaves a door unlocked. Ever. As a city cop, he's had some close brushes with some unsavory characters. If they know where you live, they'll look for any opening, right? That's how the bad guys operate."

I had never heard Jake talk like that. Something had scared him.

"So, Blake kept apologizing for the dog, saying he didn't know what was the matter, and finally decided to take him into the back bedroom. As soon as Blake left the room, I heard a knock at the door."

Jake had started to sweat. "I got up and unlocked the door, but when I looked out, I didn't immediately see anyone. It was the voice that got my attention. A kid's voice. It said, *'We need to use your phone.'*"

A Hiss

Jake licked his lips as if he had just lost all the saliva in his mouth.

I stood up and quickly got him a bottle of water from the fridge. I twisted off the cap and gave it to him.

"Thanks," he mumbled without looking at me.

I felt a cold draft. It might have been my imagination. It might have been exactly that, a cold draft. But just in case it was something else, I went and stood close to my aunt. I knew I wasn't a child anymore, but I was also one of the few adults in the world who had not just heard the things that go bump in the night but had seen them too. When my gut told me to move, I moved.

Jake pressed his lips together then reluctantly

spoke again. "I looked down and saw two kids standing at the door. Just two little kids who couldn't have been more than ten years old, standing outside the screen door. A boy and girl. They had on these weird clothes, as if they were all the same color. Like I was looking at a black-and-white movie. Only they weren't in a movie; they were right in front of me. And they had their heads down as though they were looking at something on the ground or were ready to be scolded. I don't know."

"They wanted to use the phone?" Aunt Astrid asked.

"That's what they said, but I don't really believe that was what they wanted. I think they wanted to just get inside the house."

"Why would you think that?" Bea asked. "Why would you think these little kids would just want to get inside?" The idea of sinister children was especially bothersome to Bea, I could tell. Her biological clock was ticking, and the idea that something so innocent could be terrifying would cause fear in her heart.

"Just call it a gut feeling," Jake said. "They teach us on the force to always go with that gut feeling. They told us it would save our lives more than our sidearm. If we listen to our gut, we won't have to use a sidearm. Makes sense, right? I think I've only pulled my piece from my holster, what, three times? If that." He spoke as if he didn't really want to continue. It was as if he had to relay some very bad news and wished he could just skip it.

"'*We need to use the phone. We need to call our mom.*' That was what they said. So I tried to reason that maybe they knew Blake and knew he was a detective and thought this was a safe place to ask for help. But no matter how I tried to convince myself that they were normal children, something inside me was saying shut the door."

Jake took another sip of water before continuing. "So, I reached in my pocket and took out my phone, telling them to give me their number, and when I looked at them..."

"Jake?" Bea waited for him to answer. It was as if he had suddenly changed his mind and didn't want to talk. "Jake, what is it?"

He laughed, shaking his head as if he had already given up on the idea that we would believe him and figured he had to be wrong about something or everything.

But then I saw the tear slip down his cheek from the corner of his eye. I had seen some scary things in my life. Being a witch meant sometimes I had to seek out those scary things. But if I lived to be one hundred years old, I would never see anything as scary as this grown man trembling while he told us a story he was convinced we wouldn't believe. Something had not just scared him but intentionally set out to terrify him.

"The dog was going crazy," he said. "I looked back to see if Blake was there. All I wanted was to see him down the hall or something. I just didn't want to be alone with these kids at the door. But Blake was still in the back of the house with Frank, who was still barking his head off."

He took another deep breath and looked at Bea. There was so much love there. And it seemed to me that Jake was not just looking to her for comfort, but that he needed some real help.

After all the years on the Wonder Falls Police Department, after all of his studies and training, nothing had prepared him for this. Right then, Bea was his only defense.

"When I turned back around, they were right at the screen door, looking up at me. They were staring at me. Their eyes were completely black."

"I knew it," I hissed.

"Jake, why didn't you say anything sooner?" Bea knelt down in front of him and held his hands.

He pulled one hand away quickly, wiping his eyes and smiling just a little. "Well, it isn't like forgetting to pay the gas bill or backing into a pole with the car. It's a bit more out there than what we usually talk about."

"Jake." Aunt Astrid stood up. Her face was serious. "Did they touch you?"

He shook his head hard. "Touch me? Are you crazy?"

"What did you do then?" I asked. I wanted to hear that Jake had told them in no uncertain terms that they should get the hell off the porch and never show their ugly faces again or they would risk a night in the tank. I wanted to hear a string of obscenities directed toward these little monsters that would scare them back to whatever dimension they had come from. But I didn't. What I heard made me tremble.

"They told me again to let them in. Only, it wasn't like regular voices. It was like a hiss. And it wasn't like we're talking now. It was *inside* my head."

I gasped.

Jake clenched and unclenched his fists. "And you know what the worst part was?"

"It gets worse? How can that be?" I asked, my eyes wide and my mouth hanging open.

"I didn't even realize that my hand was reaching for the latch to open the door. I was completely oblivious to it. It was like I was being pulled like a puppet."

"Oh, Jake. That's just horrible," Bea said. I could hear in her voice the compassion for Jake, but underneath that, there was an unmistakable rage. Something had messed with her man. I wasn't sure who I was more worried for, Jake or those *things* once Bea got a hold of them.

"If I had opened that door even a hair, those things would have gotten in. Not just inside Blake's house but... inside my head." Then he started to laugh out loud. "I had my phone in my hand. I swear I was about to dial 9-1-1. How would that have looked? Me calling 9-1-1 while I'm at the house of my police partner?"

I couldn't help it. That made me laugh out loud.

"But even though I was going to dial 9-1-1, my hand was shaking so bad, the numbers were all a blur. And those kids just leaned in closer to the screen, staring up at me, quietly whispering for me to let them in." Jake took both of Bea's hands in his and held them tightly. "I just thought of you, Bea. All that came to mind was your pretty face. Then I slammed the door shut. You know how it feels when you pull out a splinter or rip off a Band-Aid really fast? It hurts but feels good once it's done, right? That was how I felt. Like a thick splinter had been pulled from somewhere."

"Did they try to get in anywhere else?" I asked.

"I don't know. But after I slammed the door shut, within a couple of seconds, I heard this loud crash. You can bet I thought they had help trying to break into the back of the house while I was distracted." Jake reached behind his head and scratched Treacle, who was sitting there, listening with closed eyes. "My police training kicked in, and I drew my weapon. The dog had stopped barking. I was sure something had gotten into the house, but Blake stepped into the hallway, perfectly fine.

"He shouted at me to holster my weapon, and I asked him about the crashing sound. He didn't hear anything and just wondered who was at the door. I couldn't tell him two little kids scared the hell out of me and that I was afraid to walk to my own car." Jake looked sad. "I didn't want to say anything about this, but I haven't felt right since it all happened. Do you know what those things are? Do you know what they want?"

The room was completely silent, and that scared me.

None of us knew what those things were, but now two people had seen them. One had let them in and committed suicide the next day. The other hadn't but was suffering a severe case of Post-Traumatic Stress Disorder.

I looked at Aunt Astrid. She was the oldest of us with the most experience. She had seen it all and been around the block a few times. She had to have some memory of that type of creature or had maybe seen it skating through the dimensions as she studied them. But the studious look on her face told me she had no answer for Jake.

"I've only heard of these things, Jake," she finally said, knowing we were all looking to her for guidance. "And I've only *just* heard of them. I'm sure if we did some digging, there might be stories of them, but I don't know how much help that would be to us."

I felt a chill go across my shoulders. "Yeah. If some butter-churner in the eighteenth century saw one of these things, I don't know how much that would help us out. Maybe there is something going on at this time of year that attracts them. Like a mating season or foraging season or something." I shrugged. Everyone turned and looked at me at once. "What?" I asked. "It's just a suggestion."

"No. You might be on to something, Cath," Aunt Astrid said. "If we do a little research, we might find a pattern as to when these sightings took place, if nothing else. It's a long shot, but I think it's worth a try."

"But you are not invited," Bea said to Jake.

"What? Why? I can research a book as well as the next guy," he said, almost pouting.

"You need to rest," Bea said. "And then you need to get back on your feet and act as if nothing happened. For all we know, those things were after Blake and got you instead. Who knows what would have happened if they had hit their target."

"I didn't think of that." Jake sat back in his seat. "You're right."

I hadn't thought of that either. But I successfully hid my concern behind an awkward grimace.

Bea helped Jake get back to bed. He had worn himself out with all the talking about such a strenuous topic. When Bea came back into the kitchen, we all looked at each other.

"You know what that means?" Aunt Astrid asked Bea.

"You mean the fact that Jake heard the breaking glass?" Bea asked.

Both Aunt Astrid and I nodded.

The poor guy had already been shaken enough. Telling him that he had heard something breaking through to another dimension would have been too much for the big brute. Telling him to get used to it because he obviously had a sixth sense... well, none of us thought it was the right time at all.

But there was no doubt among us that the breaking glass sound meant those creatures were high-tailing it out of Dodge for the time being.

The real questions were: Where were they coming from? and Who was going to see them next?

Gone Fishing

✦❧✦

We had posted a sign on the door at the Brew-Ha-Ha that we had all gone fishing for the day. Life was a little too hectic for any of us to focus on work. When we returned the following day, our steady stream of regulars, and some irregulars, showed up and asked if everything was okay.

That was one of the great things about living in Wonder Falls. It wasn't a huge metropolis, but it wasn't just a hayseed town either. It was a mix of good-hearted people who got along relatively well and just a sprinkling of weirdos. My family could easily slip into the latter category.

In between saying howdy-do to the regular patrons and serving up the pastries and special dishes of the day, I was able to get a few words in to Bea.

"How's Jake feeling?" I asked.

"He's feeling a lot better. I couldn't stop him from going to work last night. He's as stubborn as a mule. And he didn't want to talk about, you know, what he told us." She looked around to make sure there weren't any prying ears.

"But," she continued, turning to me with wildly excited eyes, "there's news about the Roy case." She brought her hand up to cover her mouth so no one would see her mouth the word "Roy."

"Really?" Aunt Astrid said from behind me. "What's happening?"

"Yeah, what's happening?" I couldn't believe I had almost forgotten about my encounter with Blake at the Roy house.

"Jake said that Blake had been staking out their house just on the off chance he saw something unusual or noticed any kids lurking around up to no good. He hasn't given up on the whole black-eyed kid thing being a hoax." She looked around quickly, most likely to see if anyone from the Prestwick area was in the café.

When she didn't see any Prestwickans, she continued. "While he was sitting there, he saw a man pull up in the driveway in a beat-up blue pickup truck."

My heart froze. Had Blake mentioned he was sitting in my car with me? Had he mentioned how close we were when we ducked down in the seat to avoid being seen? I began to chew my lip nervously. My mind flashed back to those few minutes we'd been together. He'd smelled so good. I remembered seeing a little bit of a smile on his face. I thought I had. Hadn't I?

"...and answered the door with a shotgun," Bea was saying.

I guess Blake hadn't said anything about me. I wasn't sure if I was relieved or hurt.

Bea continued with the story where I had left off with Blake following the car out of Prestwick.

"Were he and Lisa having an affair?" Aunt Astrid asked. Actually, that was the first thing that had popped into my mind, and I wasn't really sure what that said about my aunt or me.

"Well, this is where it gets weird," Bea said. "It turns out the guy's name is Shawn Eshelman. He worked at the bodega in the lobby of the building John Roy's law firm was in. The Roys had some car trouble, so for a couple of weeks, Lisa drove John to work and picked him up. Every once in a while, she'd go in to wait for him in the lobby, and Shawn would see her. He'd bring her a coffee or a water and chat her up."

Bea continued. "Lisa thought he was being so nice because he knew John. That is until the day he came out of the store with a paper bag and handed it to her. Without thinking or understanding, she reached inside and pulled out a magazine. It was one of those filthy pornographic magazines they sell behind the counter."

"What?" I yelled, causing everyone in the café to turn and look at me. "I'm sorry, everyone. I just found out Bea has never seen Star Wars. I know. Shocking."

"Why do you insist on throwing me under the bus when you embarrass yourself?" Bea asked with her hand on her hip. "And I have so seen Star Wars."

"I'm sorry, Bea. I just... I just... I can't believe this story. Go on."

"Okay, but control yourself, woman."

Needless to say, Lisa had been upset by Shawn's inappropriate behavior and went right to John. He complained to the owner of the bodega and got the guy fired. But what should have been the end of the situation was just the beginning.

"Lisa was obviously unnerved by the experience.

So she stayed away from John's office. But that didn't stop this Shawn guy. He had found out where she lived and popped up in front of her at the grocery store one day.

"He kept saying he was sorry and that it was just a bad joke. Lisa thought the guy was sincere, accepted his apology and tried to go about her business. But then Shawn kept showing up at the gym and at the post office. It was getting to a point where Lisa didn't want to leave the house, but she had started to feel as though he were watching that too. He was also telling people that they were dating."

"This is like a soap opera." Aunt Astrid said.

"Right? But because he liked to talk so much, he painted himself into a corner. He was telling someone who was close to the Roys that he had been with Lisa on a particular day, and this person knew it was a bold-faced lie. The Roys had actually been with him and his wife that particular day."

"That had to shut him up." I assumed a healthy dose of humiliation would be enough for me to tuck tail and run.

"Not even close," Bea continued. "Instead of cutting his losses, he gets even nastier. The next thing the Roys know is that there are threatening notes being left at their house with obvious signs that someone was trespassing on their property. John would get weird calls at work, and of course Lisa would get them at home. But as Blake said, the guy rode a fine line between legal and illegal activities. There was nothing they could do."

"So why didn't Lisa tell the guys about this when they were interviewing her after John's death?" Aunt Astrid asked. "I don't believe this Shawn character pushed John out the window, but I wouldn't rule him out as being involved."

"Well, here is the icing on the cake," Bea said. "As it turned out, the guy had gone off his medication and was acting out. But John didn't know this. So, he paid a couple of good ol' boys to find Shawn and beat the living tar out of him with the promise they'd keep coming back as long as he did."

"Okay, now we are starting to sound like Chicago politics," I said, rolling my eyes.

"Well, maybe so. But it worked. After Shawn had his hind end handed to him, he went to the doctor and got fixed up and back on his medication. This was almost a year ago, and there had been no incident since. But when John's obit showed up in the paper, this dude wanted to offer his condolences in person. He kept calling Lisa. He sent her a couple of cards. He showed up at her house when everything else failed."

"And the man who answered the door in his sweats with a shotgun?" I asked.

"That was Lisa's uncle. We can only assume he was one of the guys who beat Shawn up—just by the way he acted and the way Shawn reacted." Bea looked at me strangely for a second. "How did you know the guy was wearing sweats?"

I stumbled and tripped over my words, sounding as though I had a stuttering problem. "I don't know. Beats me. I mean, I mean... just a guess. I mean the guy was a rural kind of fellow, right? You said it right then."

Aunt Astrid gave me a look up and down as if I might have suddenly sprouted roots for feet, and Bea looked down her nose as if there was something hiding in my hair. Then they looked at each other.

"Anyway," Bea said, a little too heavily with the attitude, "Lisa didn't bring it up because nothing had happened for months, and she didn't want anyone to think badly about John. He paid money for some guys to beat up another guy. It isn't usually how lawyers handle things. The only other people who knew about it and corroborated the facts were both their parents. Lisa wanted to make sure someone else knew just in case one or both of them disappeared."

"Good plan?" I asked, shaking my head. "How was this ruled a suicide so quickly if this Shawn guy gets dangerous if he gets off his medication? I don't know, Bea."

"Blake is still looking into things, but it looks like Shawn has been on his best behavior for months. And he also has a pretty solid alibi as to where he's been, including on the day John jumped from the window."

"I am exhausted after just hearing about all that," my aunt said. "And it still doesn't help us with the fact that two people have seen black-eyed kids and both suffered issues."

"Maybe three," I said. "Did anyone think that maybe Shawn saw something? Maybe it wasn't just being off his meds that made him crazy?"

"Perhaps we could pay Shawn a visit," Aunt Astrid said. "Bea, did the guys mention where he lives?"

"It's funny you should ask that," Bea said. "Shawn gave an address to the police of where he's living in Harrisburg. He's been there for over a year now. Before that, he said he lived in Prestwick for a couple of years, but the address he gave was for a house that was condemned over five years ago."

"Is he rich?" I asked. People didn't just decide they wanted to live in Prestwick. It had to be earned with a trust or a six-figure income.

"Nope," Bea said. "Said he rented from a guy he never met. To live in this twelve-room house by himself cost him six hundred dollars a month."

I didn't have to say it. I could see it on both Bea's and Aunt Astrid's faces. Something about this whole situation just wasn't right. Lisa's story was bizarre enough, but for this young guy to have lived in the area, renting a mansion for pennies in the vicinity of the woman he had decided to stalk, just seemed too weird.

I thought of how jigsaw puzzles were harder when all the pieces looked alike. This mystery had a dozen components, but I couldn't see how they fit. I just couldn't see anything.

Screaming

✦✦✦

A couple of days had passed since the stories with the black-eyed children and the stalking of Lisa Roy had floated to the surface. I was happy to see Jake was feeling better since his incident. He was working and feeling more like his old self. However, if he knew how much damage had been done, and what Bea had seen of the energy around his head and heart being all scratched up and beaten down, he might have succumbed to his injuries.

Seeing that kind of damage could lead a person to believe they wouldn't ever be the same. And maybe Jake wouldn't be the same after his attack. That was what had happened—he had been attacked by those things. But Bea nursed him along; she whispered her spells while he slept and watched as layer after layer of scarring was removed.

She was really good at healing, no doubt about it.

That night, it was my turn to lock up the café. The nights were getting longer with winter quickly approaching, but we still had sweater weather. I pulled my ankle-length, rust-colored sweater around me and began my walk home.

A thin veil of fog hung in the streets. It gave the streetlamps halos and softened the edges of the houses and fences I passed. Trees and shrubs morphed into giant animals, blending seamlessly with shadows that were already there.

Despite the eerie atmosphere, I felt a strange sense of calm and was enjoying the night as I turned down the street where the Greenstones all resided. I didn't care what people thought about the prestige that came with a Prestwick address. To me, having my family just a few doors down made me feel very wealthy.

I had my own little house, a little car, and a job that I didn't ever want to leave. I had clothes to stay warm, and even though I didn't cook like Bea, I could still open a can of soup and had plenty in my pantry. If only my parents could see me. If only I could let them know I had turned out okay.

I knew Aunt Astrid was probably poring over her immense library, looking for something that alluded to black-eyed children. Bea was most likely fluttering around Jake, making sure everything was back to normal and making sure the doors and windows were locked, not just with a physical latch but with a spell or two as well.

I had decided I might crack open one of those cans of soup, put on the television, and zone out to an old movie or something. I wanted to give my mind a break from all the drama that seemed to be popping up like toadstools.

But as I made the plans in my head, I noticed a familiar-looking car in my driveway. There was only one person who drove a new Jaguar and didn't live in Prestwick.

I tapped the glass on the passenger window. "What are you doing here?" I asked my dear friend Min.

He must have been really engrossed in thought because he looked as if I'd scared him out of his skin when I tapped. He climbed out of the car. Even in the pale, foggy evening, I could see there was something wrong.

"I was in the neighborhood. We hadn't had a

chance to just talk for a while. You know, just you and I. Can we go inside?"

It didn't take over a decade of friendship for me to realize Min was terribly upset but trying to keep up appearances. The first thought I had was that he and his girlfriend Amalia had called it quits.

"Well, sure. Come on in. Can I get you something to drink? I've got tea, water. Or hot chocolate with marshmallows. And no, not the cat."

Min barely chuckled and seemed awfully anxious as I pushed the front door open. Looking over his shoulder, up to the sky, then down around the shrubs near my bay window, he made it clear he had a severe case of ants in his pants.

Once inside the foyer, Min quickly turned around and shut the door behind us, slipping the deadbolt into place. Had it been anyone else but Min, I might have been nervous. But since he was my best friend, I held back and didn't hit him with a restraining spell. Such a spell would have not only frozen his muscles and reduced him to a pile of jelly on the floor, but it also would have made him lose control of his bowels. It would've been an ugly mess, but in any other situation, a girl like me would have had no choice.

He peeked out the windows, and I heard him sigh

as he kicked off his shoes, an Asian tradition. Just then, I heard the familiar scratching sound coming from the kitchen window.

"Who's scratching out there?" I said loudly, out of habit, while walking to the kitchen window.

"No! Don't open it!" Min shouted at the top of his lungs, making both Treacle and me jump out of our skin.

Opening the window, I turned to Min. "What is the matter with you?" I barked, more out of shock than anger. "It's just the cat!"

"I'm sorry. I'm so sorry. I didn't know it was the cat. I'm sorry, Treacle," Min said, reaching down to pet the furry beast that quickly slid away from his hand and instead circled my legs.

"It's okay, Min. Sit down. Hot chocolate it is. You look like you need it."

"What's his problem?" Treacle asked.

"Don't know yet," I replied in my mind.

I shut the window and went to my pantry to pull out two packets of instant hot chocolate. While I took the tea kettle to heat some water, Min stepped over to the window and gave it a good tug to make sure it was closed all the way.

I didn't say anything about it. Instead, I yanked the refrigerator door open and grabbed the milk.

Other than a half-opened can of cat food, a withered head of lettuce, and some eggs, I had absolutely no food in the house. I could have offered Min some crackers, but I was pretty sure they were stale.

"Okay, Min. What's the matter?"

He sat down at my small kitchen table that had two mismatched chairs arranged across from each other. In the middle of the table was a small wooden bowl with daintily wrapped bundles of sage that I thought made the kitchen smell earthy and welcoming.

Min cleared his throat and fiddled with his hands. He leaned both elbows on the table and took a big breath, but still nothing came out.

Finally, I put my hand on his arm and spoke. "Min, you can talk to me."

He seemed to settle and took my hand in his. I could feel him trembling just a little. What the heck was this all about?

"We've been friends for a long time, right?" he asked.

"Best of friends, Min. You know that."

"If I told you something and asked you not to tell anyone else, I could trust you, right?"

"Of course you could, Min. Not a word to

anyone." I looked him in his eyes. "It's always been that way."

He nodded as if he already knew that. "But if I told you something that wasn't normal, that was just impossible to believe, you wouldn't judge me, right? Or my mom?"

I sat back in my chair. This was obviously more serious than a breakup.

"I love your family, Min. I know what kind of people they are. Nothing anyone could say or do would ever change that."

He looked away for a second. It was as if he was studying the tile on the floor or looking for some cheat sheet down there that might give him an answer to a question he didn't know how to ask.

"What's the matter?"

Min took a deep breath and finally began to talk. He had gone to his parents' house for a visit. Work had kept him kind of busy, and when he wasn't working, he was spending time with Amalia. So he bought some fried chicken, which he knew both his parents loved, and headed over to their house.

As usual, Mr. Park was at his store, where he would be until closing around eleven thirty at night. Min told his mother he would hang around and visit until his father was home.

They had just finished eating when there was a loud knock on the door.

Thump. Thump. Thump.

"Are you expecting anyone?" Min had asked his mother who, with a mouthful of fried chicken, shook her head.

Walking quietly through the living room from the kitchen in bare feet, Min got to the door and opened it. There was no one there. He stepped out into the cool evening air and looked around, but not so much as a leaf rustled in a tree. He was just about to step off the porch and look around the side of the house when he heard his mother. She was screaming.

Let Me In

✤

"She was terrified," Min said. "I didn't know what could have scared her so much, but I ran back into the kitchen. She had tears in her eyes and was pointing at the window, still yelling."

The tea kettle began to whistle, and both of us nearly jumped out of our own skin. I stood up, looking toward the window that I'd let Treacle in, remembering Min had locked it tightly behind me.

"Here," I said, pouring the hot liquid into our cups along with a splash of milk and a handful of mini marshmallows each. "A spoon full of sugar," I said before setting the kettle back on the stove and taking my seat again.

Min wrapped his hands around the mug and continued his story.

His mother had begun to back out of the kitchen when Min tried desperately to get her to tell him what was the matter. Finally, he looked where she was pointing, and there in the window, staring in at them, had been two pale-faced children with jet-black eyes.

"I know what you're thinking," Min said. "That they were children with contact lenses. They were playing a joke and just causing mischief." He swallowed hard and looked at me. "They were not children."

He went on to say that he'd had a strange sensation spread over him. Never in his life had a terror settled so deep into his bones that he was afraid it might never come out. "There was something in their eyes, Cath. It was like a vacuum. It sucked me in, and the terror was so intense, it was crippling."

He could no longer hear his mother, who had still been crying and screaming. Instead, he said his head was filled with whispers—childlike hissing whispers that didn't sound like children talking quietly, but rather how one would imagine conspiring demons sounded.

With a snap in his brain like a mousetrap being set off, he remembered the front door.

As if reading his mind, the children disappeared from the window with insane speed. In his gut, Min felt they were headed back around to the open door. He had left it wide open when he'd heard his mother scream.

"I turned and ran from the kitchen to the front door, and I saw one of them," he said. "You know how spiders run back and forth when you're trying to swat them with a broom?" The image gave me shivers. "Well, that is how one of them was moving. It was a little boy around ten years old, and he was hunched over, crawling on the tips of his fingers and the balls of his feet, back and forth on the porch like there was some invisible thing in the way of him getting into the house."

Then Min said it had stopped and looked at him, hissing. But he couldn't be sure if it had really been making noise or if it had just been in his head.

"Then, as clear as I'm talking to you, I heard it say 'let me in.' Except it was in my head. It was in my head, Cath."

I patted Min's arm. He looked like Jake had looked when he'd spilled his guts about the same two brats showing up at Blake's place.

"And even though no words came out of my mouth, at least I'm pretty sure that none did, that thing was slowly reaching into the house. As if I were slowly giving it permission to do so. I don't know where I got the strength, but I tore my feet loose, squeezed my eyes closed, and charged the door, slamming it shut. I was sure when I finally opened my eyes, I was going to see a severed child's arm lying on the floor, but I didn't. I looked out the peephole and saw nothing on the porch. But I heard it scream. At least, I think it was a scream."

I couldn't believe this. I didn't know what to do.

"I locked the front door and hurried to my mom, who had calmed down a good bit but was shaking at the table."

"Did you ask her what she thought they were?"

"Yeah. I asked her. And her reply was Korean for 'demon.'"

Min and I sat there for a few minutes, letting it all sink in. Treacle rubbed along Min's leg as if to say *there, there*. The kind gesture brought Treacle a gentle scratching on the top of his head from Min and a little taste of marshmallow from the tip of Min's finger. That was all it took, and my favorite beast was up on the table, sitting like royalty, waiting for more scratches behind the ear to commence. He purred contentedly as Min petted him gently.

"Min, you left your mom alone. Do you think she's all right?"

"She called my father and told him what had happened."

My face must have looked shocked because Min clarified that quickly.

"She told him someone was looking in the windows and knocking on the doors. He was on his way home when I left."

"Are you going to tell him the truth?"

"I'll leave that up to my mom. My father is a reasonable man. When something strange or out of the ordinary happens, he will find the source, and if he can't do that, he'll pretend the whole thing never happened."

I smiled and nodded at Min. I was torn. I wasn't sure if I should tell him about Jake and John Roy or if it would be best to keep the information to myself. One thing I found interesting was that these creatures preferred to scare men, and that was not how the universe usually worked. Mrs. Park seemed to be an afterthought or perhaps an unexpected guest.

Now before I ruffle any feathers, I didn't mean to say women are weak. But there is no denying biology that dictates men are physically stronger than women. Through history men have been the warriors and protectors. How much more intense would an experience have to be to instill this kind of fear in a man?

It wasn't easy, but I knew I had to tell Aunt Astrid and Bea about Min's experience sooner rather than later. But I didn't know what to do with Min right then.

"Hey, if you're that shaken, you can stay overnight here," I said.

Min looked at me as if he had been thinking the same thing but was afraid to say anything. "Are you sure?"

"My gosh, Min, of course. Do you want to call Amalia? Let her know where you are in case she's looking for you?" I thought that would be a good way to keep things friendly and dispel any rumors that would inevitably have taken root if not tended to right away.

"She's pulling a double shift again," he said. "I can't talk to her when she's doing that because she's either busy working, or she's getting forty winks."

I nodded in understanding.

"I know it sounds crazy, Cath." Min's voice was low and embarrassed. "The truth is I'm scared to even walk to my car. And the idea of driving alone right now is just too much. Isn't this stupid? If I didn't have my mother to corroborate my story, I'd think I was losing my mind."

"Well, you know, Min, the world is filled with all kinds of anomalies. And depending on what you're willing to open your mind to, there can be all kinds of dimensions and realms. It's a real possibility that there are ghosts and demons and angels and vampires and... witches. They could all be real. They probably are real because those stories came from somewhere, right?"

I looked at him, waiting for him to agree.

He paused for a moment as if he were seriously considering the possibilities. But then a determined look crossed his face. "No, that's not how it is. There has to be an explanation. You know, Cath, maybe I am just overreacting. They were probably kids pulling a mean, cruel joke, thinking my mom was home alone."

I could tell he was really trying to convince himself of that—that it had to be a prank, and there was no such thing as ghosts or vampires or witches.

"I'm sorry, Cath. You have got to think I am the biggest baby. I appreciate your offering to let me stay, but I'm okay now. I'm going to go home and check on my mom."

"Okay," I said, a little let down. Min was such a good guy, and we had such a history together. But after his experience that day, if I were to reveal I was a bona fide witch, I thought he would never speak to me again. Because if I were a real witch, then those children could have really been demons, and if they existed, what other nightmares were out there, just waiting to jump out at Min? No, I couldn't say anything.

"Hey," Min said. "Let's get together soon and catch a movie or something."

"Yes, and please tell Amalia I need to make a trip to the art supply store soon, and I'd like her to come with."

Min nodded as he got up from his seat at the kitchen table and went to the foyer. While slipping on his shoes, he looked at me a bit awkwardly. "Cath, what do you think it was? Do you think they were kids playing a joke?"

No, Min. I think they're demons looking to steal your soul and drive you to kill yourself. That is what I think.

"Probably, Min. What else could it be, right?"

What else was I supposed say?

We hugged goodnight, and I watched from the

door as he got safely into his car. The fog had lifted, and the street was slick but clear. Min flashed his high beams at me as he backed out of the drive, and I waved. I shut the door tightly and snapped the deadbolt into place, then I went and checked all the windows, making sure they were securely locked. Better safe than sorry.

Aunt Astrid's spell of protection was pretty strong, but she had said something had used a corner of it as a chew toy. Something wanted in but wasn't able to break through.

Treacle watched me make the rounds, his green eyes following me everywhere, his ears twisting and twitching as he listened for mice in the walls, sirens outside, or the furnace kicking on.

"If only I knew where they'd show up next," I said to him as I scooped him up in my arms and carried him to the bed. *"But they seem to just be popping up at random. Figures the little monsters wouldn't play fair."*

"I stay away from children of all kinds whether they have black eyes or not." Treacle purred as I got under the covers.

"Why is that?"

"They smell funny," he said.

I looked at him as if to say he was Mr. Pot calling Miss Kettle black. *"Well, that might be,"* I said. *"Have you heard anything around town about black-eyed kids making house calls?"*

"No. Nothing at all."

"You'll let me know if you do?"

"Of course, Cath." Then Treacle licked my nose with his rough, scratchy tongue and gave me a head butt of affection before curling up and lying down next to me.

We slept through the rest of the night, and I didn't dream.

Nucleus

T he next day, my aunt came shuffling into the café with a stack of papers stuffed underneath one arm and a very unhappy-looking Marshmallow in the other. Her hair was wild, pointing in all directions as if she had gotten caught in a wind tunnel, and she was wearing the same pretty purple outfit she'd worn the day before. Except it was more wrinkled.

"Good morning, Mom. I was starting to worry." Bea looked her mother up and down just like I was doing. "Are you okay?"

"Yes," she said excitedly, handing Marshmallow to me.

"*What's this all about?*" I asked the pug-nosed cat.

"*Something about maps. She was up all night. Every*

time I found some crinkly, comfy spot to sit on her books, she'd move them. It was very annoying."

"What's all that, Aunt Astrid?" I asked, stroking Marshmallow as she purred contentedly in my arms.

"A break. The one we've been looking for." Her bright eyes twinkled. She walked around the counter to the larger table in the back of the café where she normally did her palm readings for customers.

I walked over to an empty table for two and set Marshmallow on top of it, underneath the painting of a noble cat that hung on the wall. I got her a small saucer of cream and told her I hoped it made up for the inconvenience.

"It'll do for now," she purred.

While Bea and I tended to the dwindling morning crowd, Aunt Astrid spread out her papers and mumbled to herself.

Finally, Bea and I made our way to the back table and saw a dozen old pages of text, a few weird charts that only Albert Einstein might have been able to decipher, and three old maps of Wonder Falls in various stages of development over the past couple of decades.

"So, as I was researching our dark-eyed intruders, I became very frustrated at the lack of information on them," Aunt Astrid said. "It seems no one knows anything more than we do. They're creepy. They scare the living heck out of everyone who encounters them. Their appearance and the words they speak change only slightly. But that's it." She shuffled some of the pages then sat down.

"But I found a pattern," she said proudly.

"Let me guess. They only visit men. I thought of that last night. Remind me to tell you that Min saw them too. At his mother's house." I just blurted it out. Heaven knew I wanted to keep Min's secret, but this was too important. "That just narrows it down to half of Wonder Falls. What are you looking at?" I asked both Bea and my aunt.

"Yes, you'll have to tell us about Min," Aunt Astrid said. "But can I finish first?"

"Please. I'm waiting," I said sarcastically, bumping Bea with my hip as she shook her head, giggling.

"I found that for the past seven years, there has been at least one suicide every year, all at this time of year."

I wasn't prepared for that. That wasn't at all what I was thinking, and it made my stomach queasy. A rash of suicides around Halloween? That was so sad. I clutched my throat and listened.

"Suicides?" Bea asked.

"Yes. Now, I won't bore you both with the long-drawn-out details, but it's what we've been hearing for the past couple of days, repeating itself. At the same time people claimed to see these children, someone would end their own life."

"You mean anyone who saw these black-eyed children killed themselves?" Bea asked as her face went as white as a ghost. I knew she was thinking about Jake.

"No. No, Bea. That isn't what I mean," my aunt said. "If everyone who saw these children killed themselves, we wouldn't know about them, correct? Because all the people they visited would be dead. No. People saw them. People reported seeing them. But what I think, what I'm guessing, is that anyone who let them in like Lisa Roy said John Roy had done, those are the ones that end their lives."

"But you can't be sure, can you?" Bea asked nervously.

"I can't be sure," Aunt Astrid said. "But what I am sure of is that no one—whether they saw these creatures, let them in the house, or didn't—they didn't have you there to nurse them back to health. Remember that, Bea. Remember your gift and how you used it for Jake."

Bea nodded, trying to put on a brave face that

said she believed her mother. But the glint of tears in her eyes said otherwise.

"Do you have any idea why they seem to focus on men?" I asked.

"Well, I've read some stories about women being terrified by them, but all I can think is that if these creatures feed off of fear... well, let's face it. Cath, you'd be just as terrified of a spider in the shower as you would these things."

I nodded in agreement looking at Aunt Astrid and then Bea. "Probably."

"So, my theory is that men are harder to scare. They're just hardwired to be brave in certain instances. They will automatically look for a reason or answer to something abnormal." Aunt Astrid wiped her hands on her skirt. "If you can scare them to the point of ending their own lives, well, I just think there must be a bigger payoff, more food or more energy."

"Is it just me, or does everyone in this room feel a little superior right now?" I asked.

Bea nodded, squaring her shoulders. "I do. Yes."

"Calm down, you two. It doesn't mean we can't be attacked too. It just means they prefer machismo. And it's machismo in a certain area."

"Okay. You've found a pattern in these suicides.

What does that tell us?" I asked, hoping that if we let Aunt Astrid continue, there would be some shred of hope that those things weren't messengers of imminent death.

"It just turned out that the first two deaths recorded were on streets that still exist today. So I marked them on the first map. The others were on streets that have since been renamed, but look at this." She pulled out all three maps. They were of the same areas in Wonder Falls, but each map became more and more detailed.

More streets were illustrated. The district lines were changed. But the odd thing was that all Aunt Astrid's little red ticks where a suicide was reported to have happened were all in the same vicinity.

"It's like a coup of circles," I said. "And they don't seem to vary too much."

"Exactly," my aunt said. "There is something strange about this area, and I haven't yet figured it out."

"Wait." Bea looked at the maps. "What's this?" She pointed to an area on each of the maps that was wide open. "It looks like the system has a nucleus."

Did I ever mention that Bea is smart? She was really smart. And at that moment, I was shocked by her brilliance as we stared at a perfect starting point.

"That is a place in Prestwick," I said. "See, Darla lives in Prestwick, and so all kinds of evil is attracted to the place. We ought to just run her out of town." I didn't mean for the words to just fall out of my mouth.

Bea chuckled and rolled her eyes.

"What?" I asked.

"Why do you hate her again?"

I shook my head. "How much time have you got?"

"We need to find out that address and pay the owner a visit," Aunt Astrid said. "Perhaps they're conjuring something they can't control anymore."

As I studied the map, I realized that the place we were looking for used to be on Davis Street. But after a couple of years of renovation and reconstruction, the street was changed to Butternut Drive. I knew that place. With all my heart, I knew it was the place with the long driveway and the For Sale and Keep Out signs posted along the way.

But how could I tell Bea and Aunt Astrid without letting them know I went snooping and that it led to time alone in the car with Detective Samberg? It was just too humiliating for me to say. And yet, it could be helpful. The lives of innocent people could be at stake.

"So I think that I know where..."

"Oh my gosh!" Bea cried out, slapping her forehead as if she had just dropped her keys down a manhole. "Butternut Drive. That is where that Shawn Eshelman said he lived when he had gotten off his meds. It was the six-hundred-dollar-a-month mansion for one bachelor to live in. I knew that looked familiar. Jake had said that was where Shawn said he lived."

"He also said he was renting it from someone he never met, right?" I asked. "And now that house is condemned, right?"

Bea shrugged. "That's what Jake said. We need to go check that place out."

"All of us?" I asked.

"Well, what were you thinking, honey?" Aunt Astrid asked.

"Oh, well, I was just thinking that it might be better if we, you know, leave this investigating to the experts. I could tell Detective Samberg that it might be worth checking out, and I could go with him so you guys could..."

"Could what? Could wait and see if we never hear from you again? No way, girlie." Bea folded her arms across her chest and shook her head. "You know how much stronger we are together. I have the feeling we are all going to need to stick together from now on if we're going to get into this any deeper."

I shrugged. "Sure. Yeah, you're right. I was just thinking out loud."

"Just thinking out loud?" Aunt Astrid eyeballed me as if she were a teacher who had caught a student passing a note.

Just then the bell over the door jingled, and I left my two relatives to talk amongst themselves.

The customer stepped around the corner, and my breath caught in my chest. It was none other than Detective Samberg. He looked very serious, and I realized there was no Jake with him.

"Hi. Is everything okay? Is Jake all right?" I asked, getting ready to scream for Bea.

"Yeah, he's back at the station doing some paperwork."

I let my breath out and put my hands on my hips. "Then what can I do for you? Would you like a hot tea or maybe a slice of Dutch apple pie?"

"No. I'm actually here to see you."

"Me?" So yes, I was a little surprised and almost giggled. "What about?"

"Last night. Min Park was at your place, right?"

I blinked at him and tilted my head. "How do you know that?"

"His father, Mr. Park, had called the police station to say that his wife and son had seen someone trying to get into their house. Mrs. Park said Min had chased them off. But he didn't stick around to give a statement. I just find that odd."

"I don't know what's so odd about that?"

"Would you leave your aunt alone like that after witnessing someone trying to get into her house?"

Pal, you have no idea how my aunt could squeeze the stuffing right out of you before you could say "freeze, hands up."

"If my aunt said she was okay and didn't need me," I said.

"And then Min shows up at your house and stays…"

"How do you know he was at my house?" My blood was starting to boil. I couldn't believe I thought it would be a good idea to ride to Butternut Drive with this guy. What had I been thinking?

"I dropped Jake off after our shift at eleven o'clock. I saw Min's car there."

"And so what did you do?" I asked. "Just sit there and watch how long he hung out at my house?"

"I just observed something I thought was a little interesting. That's all."

I swore Blake was enjoying this. He loved to make people squirm. It was going to be one of those days that he put a gold star on his calendar. *Made that smarty pants Cath Greenstone really uncomfortable. Yay for me! Gold star!*

"Well, I was unaware that a grown woman my age had to clear it with the Wonder Falls P.D. if I wanted to have a friend come visit."

"What did you and Mr. Park talk about?" he asked.

"Nothing. We've been friends since grade school. We talk about anything and everything, if you must know."

"You mean he didn't mention anything about being with his mother and some kids with black eyes trying to get into their house?"

"Well, I don't really remember. I mean we talked about a lot of stuff and..." I was rambling, and I knew it. And I knew Blake knew it too. But how could I tell him that Min had told me this bizarre story and that I believed him one hundred percent? Blake obviously didn't know that his own partner saw these same things and practically took a bullet for Blake by answering his door.

Blake Samberg was never going to know that he might have died that night had it not been for Jake. He would never know that Min was telling the truth and so was his mother.

But I'd promised. I'd promised not to tell Min's story, and I'd also said I would keep a lid on it for Jake too.

"You don't remember him saying anything about children with black eyes showing up to peek in their windows?" Blake asked, looking down at his pocket notebook.

"I remember him saying some kids were playing a joke. Halloween is right around the corner. He did say it scared his mom, and he was a little nervous." I watched Blake's face and thought I had pulled off. I thought he wouldn't ask me anything else.

But I couldn't stop talking. "If I could make one suggestion? The next time you decide it's necessary to spy on my house, just come knock on the door. Don't stand out there lurking around like some transient."

He looked as if I had just told him to shut up and get out. For a second, I felt guilty. But it passed.

"Hello, Blake," Aunt Astrid said as if he were her long-lost son. "Can we help you with anything?"

"No, ma'am. I've got what I came for." And yes, he looked at me with a smirk when he said that.

"You look a little pale. Let me give you something for the drive back to the station." Aunt Astrid turned around and not only gave him a huge slice of Dutch apple pie, but also a gourmet salad filled with all kinds of healthy, crunchy greens, dried berries, and stuff I'd never eat but that looked delicious. She dropped it all in a bag and handed to him.

"Thanks, ma'am. I appreciate it." Then, he did the unthinkable. He looked me up and down. As if that weren't embarrassing enough, my aunt saw it and giggled. Then he turned and walked out as if he hadn't even spoken to me.

I felt eyes on me, and for a split second, I hoped it was some black-eyed children, but it wasn't. It was my aunt, smiling.

"What?" I asked.

She shook her head back and forth but said nothing as she went back to the table around the counter where Bea was still studying all the maps and notes.

Butternut

I was a bit relieved that Bea knew where the strange house in Prestwick was. After we piled into Bea's car that evening after work, we took a nice drive to Prestwick. Thankfully, the café had been slow, and we were able to close up a little early, leaving the sun hanging in the sky for at least another good two hours.

After some Google Maps searches that yielded three different routes and a few complicated turns down the serpentine roads, I couldn't help but feel a slight case of déjà vu. The fall leaves were still in colorful canopies overhead, and the houses looked even more beautiful this time since I had a chance to really look at them.

When we passed by Darla's house, I tried to look

away, but I caught sight of her standing outside. She was chatting up some guy in a van that had J&J Plumbing stenciled on the side. He was practically falling out of the driver's side window as she talked and flipped her hair. I kept my mouth shut, but I looked away in disgust, rolling my eyes and wondering how so many guys fell for her babe-in-the-woods act. When I looked in the rearview mirror, I saw Bea looking at me. She smiled and winked at me, and I smiled back.

"Okay, we need to take a left up ahead, then a quick right, and we should be just about there," Aunt Astrid said, navigating between two maps and a set of handwritten directions she had made for herself.

After a few more minutes, Bea pointed out her window.

"Is that it?" she asked. "I don't see any numbers, but that looks like a driveway. At least, I think it is. It isn't a road, right?"

"Well, let's see. The house next door was 3490 Butternut. We're looking for what?" Aunt Astrid looked at her notes. "This says 3494."

"Let's give it a try," I said, knowing it was the right place.

Bea turned and headed down the cobblestone

driveway, past the For Sale and No Trespassing signs, only to have the journey end at the wrought iron gate I had come to just a few days earlier. From that point on, I was as clueless as the other two Greenstone women. We had no idea what was up ahead.

"You feel that?" I asked as I opened the car door.

"Yeah." Bea nodded as she climbed out from behind the wheel. "Like someone blasting a boom box or subwoofers on their car."

"Something is here," Aunt Astrid said.

I stretched my legs and my back as I looked around.

"Everyone smile. We're on camera," I said as casually as possible, motioning in the general direction of a camera at the far corner of the fence and then at one pointed down on the driveway from a tall tree.

"Well, at least we know someone is watching the place," Aunt Astrid said, looking not only at the camera but past it and through it, trying to see the person who had installed them.

"Maybe," Bea said. "They look pretty old and neglected. Big, bulky things from the seventies or something."

They did look pretty old, but I wasn't sure they

were inoperable. They might have looked that way on purpose.

My aunt was gently waving her hands as if she were performing some kind of exercise or pushing invisible curtains aside, which she probably was.

"Maybe we should make an appointment like we're interested in the property," Bea said. "That way, we wouldn't have to trespass in order to get a look around. We're just a couple of ladies looking to invest in a bigger house where we could all take care of the frail and ailing Astrid Greenstone." Bea looked playfully at her mom. "Besides, if those cameras *do* work and we sneak in, how would it look if Detective Jake Williams had to not only bail his wife out of the clink, but his mother-in-law and cousin-in-law too?"

"Yeah, that would look pretty bad," I chuckled. "Good call, Bumble Bea. I'll make the appointment."

Aunt Astrid didn't reply. She didn't laugh. She just stood there, looking through the fence bars, and I could only imagine what other layers of reality.

Her face was firm and set in a stare far off down the driveway past the gate. "We're being watched."

Bea stepped closer to her mother. "What do you see?"

"Black eyes," Aunt Astrid said, her voice low and firm. "Maybe four sets. Six at the most." She squinted and stepped up to the metal gate, wrapping her hands around the bars and looking in. "They don't like us being here. Not one bit."

"Can they tell we're witches?" I asked. I wasn't sure if we gave off some kind of paranormal aroma or glowed like a road flare because of our connection with the magical.

"I don't know," my aunt said. "I don't think it matters. They don't look like they'd be happy with anyone showing up. Equal-opportunity haters."

Bea squinted, looking behind us, back the way we had come down the driveway.

"We need to get into the house." She walked to her car and opened the door. She came back with a wrinkled receipt and a pen and wrote down the number on the faded For Sale sign.

"That's going to take time," I said. "We have to be fit into the agent's schedule. They have to meet us here and walk through the place with us. It's going to be a big hassle. But look." I walked up to the gate and pushed hard, stretching the chain. "We could squeeze through here and make our way down to the—"

Something screamed.

"Okay! I heard that! Did you guys hear that? Tell me you heard that," I said to the ladies as I slowly let go and backed away from the gate. "You did hear that, right?"

"I heard it," Bea said, taking her mother's hand and pulling her away from the rusted gate.

"No," Aunt Astrid whispered as she pointed. "They aren't happy we're here at all."

"Okay, then I think it's time to go," I said. "We can come back with permission and be a little better prepared, with pepper spray and weapons and a couple of layers of protection spells, along with a few surprises like lightning bolts and binding incantations."

"Yes, hurry." My aunt backed up. "Something is coming."

It didn't take much for all of us to pile back into Bea's car like a bunch of circus clowns. Just as we shut the doors, the wind whipped up something fierce.

They hadn't been there a second ago. But they were just a couple of yards in front of us now. Three pale-faced children. Staring. I didn't just see hatred in those jet-black eyes, but a hunger that terrified me. Smiles loaded with some kind of feral insanity spread across their faces. I was beginning to doubt the distance between us and wondered if the barrier of the glass and steel of the car was enough to protect us.

"I see them," I said without moving my lips. "Three creepy kids over there. Yeah, I see them."

"I do too," Bea said while turning the key in the ignition.

I was never so happy to hear a car roar to life as I was at that minute. Before I could say anything, Bea hit the gas and peeled out of the driveway backwards. As fast as we moved, the creepy children were a little quicker. Within a blink, they were at the gate with their pale hands wrapped around the bars and their eyes glaring at us.

With some quick maneuvers, Bea got us down the driveway and back onto Butternut Drive, heading away from that house.

"If we're going to go into that house, we'll need protection, and that will take a few days to prepare," my aunt said.

Hearing those words, I snapped my head in her direction. "We're still going in there? Really?" I laughed nervously.

"Cath, who knows who they might come after next?" Bea asked. "They might try and finish what they started with Jake or Detective Samberg. Who knows? We've got to stop them."

"Bea is right," Aunt Astrid said. "They can't be reasoned with. They can't feel compassion. They are evil things."

I knew they were right. But something in my gut was trying to tell me this was more than a couple of pesky entities. Maybe I found the whole thing so upsetting because they were children. But they weren't children. They were taking the form of children. Little kids didn't make a person kill themselves. Maybe children were brats sometimes, but they weren't deadly.

Despite all the rational thoughts in my head, my gut kept twisting as if I were missing something staring right at me. I remembered Jake's words about trusting his gut, and I felt really afraid.

Mysterious Creatures

＊＊＊

I t was still so early in the evening that we all regrouped back at Bea's house.

Jake had already headed off to work. The house was quiet except for Peanut Butter, who greeted us with a stern look.

"What's happening?" he asked.

"Oh, you know, the usual. Creepy spirits. Mysterious creatures. For us, that is just another day on the farm." I reached down to scratch his head as I passed.

Bea scooped the kitty up from the floor, and we all went into the kitchen without saying a word.

I took my usual seat at the end of the counter as Bea quietly cut up some apples, got some cheese out of the fridge, and tore a loaf of day-old bread from the café into small pieces, piling it all on a plate for us to eat.

Surprisingly, after such a gut-wrenching excursion, I found myself gobbling up the stuff, even the healthy apples that I usually shied away from.

"Someday you're going to cook hamburgers for me for breakfast, aren't you, Bea?" I asked, trying to break the silence with a little humor.

She smiled and winked at me.

"Okay," I said. "I'll call the real estate agent and schedule us an appointment to get into that house. But I'm going to schedule it for the first thing in the morning. I mean as soon as the sun is up. I'm not taking a chance that we'll get stuck out there in the dark." I shivered at the thought of being there again with the sun sinking and shadows getting longer.

"I'm going to check into the history of that place," Aunt Astrid said. She hadn't touched any of her food. "Maybe there was something done on that property that has attracted those creatures. Knowing that might give us a slight advantage."

"I'll check with Jake and see if he learned anything else from Mr. Eshelman when he lived there," Bea added. "I have the feeling he would have stayed on his medication had he not been staying in that house."

After we all had our own tasks assigned, we sat there without speaking.

"What's going on?" Bea finally asked. "We're never this quiet. After an experience like that, we're usually like a couple of blue jays, hawking it up."

"I was thinking that too," I said.

Aunt Astrid, who still looked very stern and had not relaxed since we left that house, shook her head slowly from side to side. "I don't know, girls. I don't know what it is."

Aunt Astrid didn't know what it was? She didn't have an answer for us? She didn't have a theory? What kind of alternate universe had we stepped into? This scared me even more than the black-eyed children.

I couldn't explain it, but I wanted to be home in my house. I wanted to be alone.

After I walked my aunt to her home, she went to the window and watched me get inside my house without incident. The familiar scratch was not at the window that night. Treacle had obviously found something interesting to keep him out a little longer.

I took one of the bundles of sage from my kitchen table, inhaled it deeply, and felt its soothing effect. I lit the dried herbs in a small bowl with pretty pink flowers around the edges and let the smoke surround me. Then I took it from room to room, just in case. To be on the safe side, I said the cleansing incantation that I had learned from my aunt when I'd first moved out on my own.

"You don't know how other people have treated the property before you. Fill it with light and positive energy right away and reapply as needed." I remembered Aunt Astrid saying that with a smile and a tear in her eye.

I had moved out of her home when I was nineteen to live in my parents' old house. She'd still had Bea with her, but she and Jake were on the fast track to matrimony. It was only a matter of time before Aunt Astrid would have her big home all to herself.

But, as if the stars had aligned themselves for a purpose, the Brew-Ha-Ha began turning a good profit, and Bea and Jake had bought a house on our block.

And we both did our sage cleansings. Aunt Astrid put up protection spells with the help of the cats. So far, all had been safe and sound up until that moment when we were all feeling the need to isolate ourselves within the walls of our homes.

"That's it," I mumbled out loud to myself. "Isolation is one of the first things people do when they start to get depressed." I waved the sage around more and more. I burnt the leaves and let the smoke reach every corner of the house. With each breath, my head felt clearer and clearer.

"They put the whammy on us," I said out loud. "Those little brats got to us from that far away. They got inside our heads, and they followed us home."

My house was so full of the sage smoke, I was sure the fire alarms were going to go off. Once I was finished, I breathed deeply. It was as if I had taken a long nap and felt refreshed and awake.

I heard scratching on my window. I thought it was Treacle, and I pulled the curtain aside and reached for the latch, only to see four jet-black eyes staring in at me.

"Whoa!" I yelled, backing away from the glass. They thought they would be able to get in. I didn't look at their eyes. Instead, I focused on the point between their eyes. It was hard to do, but I knew if I looked into that blackness, I would be a goner.

"You aren't welcome here! The stars and the moon see your deeds! By the four winds, I command you to leave this place!" I took a shaky step closer to the window. "I said, leave this place and don't come back!"

All they did was scowl at me. Their sinister

mouths pulled into painful and distorted grimaces, but I stood firm.

"Leave this place! You are not welcome!"

As quickly as they were there, they were gone. I had no time to lose. I grabbed my remaining bundles of sage from the kitchen table and ran across the street. I pounded on my aunt's door then fumbled with my keys and let myself in.

"What is the matter with you?" she asked, emerging from her bathroom with soap on her face.

"I don't have time to explain. Here. Burn this. Burn it right now and do the incantation you taught me."

"But Cath, I have a protection spell on the—"

"Please, Aunt Astrid! Just trust me and do it. I have to get to Bea." I slammed the door shut behind me and ran the few houses down to Bea's place.

I rang the bell and banged on the door so hard that I was sure one of the neighbors would call the cops and send Jake speeding over here. Finally, when she didn't answer, I let myself in.

"Bea!"

She still didn't respond.

"Bea!"

Nothing.

I called Peanut Butter in my mind, but he didn't

reply either. I bound up the stairs and found Bea lying on the bed, sobbing. Peanut Butter was huddled in the corner and looked afraid to move.

"Cath, what's wrong with Mom?" he asked, and my heart just broke for him.

"She's got a germ," I said bitterly. *"She'll be all right in a few minutes. You just come and stay close to me."*

"Bea. Hey, Bumble Bea, come on. Snap out of it," I said while I lit the sage.

"Jake called," she said. "Another man tried to kill himself tonight. His name was Monty Krueger. He tried to hang himself from a tree in his front yard."

"Bea, you need to inhale some of this. Sit up, girl." I gently blew the smoke over her body and waved it into the air.

"Feel that?" I asked Peanut Butter. *"Feel that change in the air?"*

"Yes, I do."

"Something followed us home from that house, and it's making your mom see nothing but bad things. This will help. And you just curl up with her. That will help too."

Peanut Butter was all too happy to do as I said. He snuggled up to Bea, but she just lay there. She stared ahead with red eyes, crying for a Mr. Krueger that Jake had told her about.

"Just take a couple deep breaths. You'll feel better

in a few minutes. Trust me." I blew on the embers until they glowed white and waved the smoke throughout the entire room.

"Bea? How you doin' over there?" I looked at her as she reached down to pet Peanut Butter, who was purring loudly.

"Keep it up," I said to the cat. *"I'll be right back."*

I don't know if it was because Bea was a healer or if it was just because she was a downright good person, but whatever whammy those little beasties had put on Aunt Astrid and me seemed to especially get her against the ropes.

Quickly, I went through the house. I recited the incantation over and over, making sure the sage fumes reached every corner. Finally, when I had cleansed every part of the house and even the basement, I charged back up to Bea's bedroom. She was sitting up, her face in her hands.

"Bea? You feeling better?"

Peanut Butter was on her lap.

"Yes," she said weakly. When she looked up at me, I could see she had stopped crying. "What the heck, Cath?"

"Those kids did something to us. I don't know what. But if we weren't Greenstones, I think that we'd all have been found dead tomorrow. Suicide.

And since we're family, can you imagine the kinds of gossip would go around? My gosh, Aunt Astrid's library alone would be enough for everyone to assume we'd made some pact with the devil."

Bea chuckled, but then her eyes widened with worry. "My mom!"

"It's okay. I already stopped there. She's all right and burning her sage too." Sitting down on the bed next to Bea, I put my arm around her.

"What made you think of it, Cath? The sage, I mean."

"I don't know. When I got home, I was feeling the weight of the world, and it just seemed to call to me, you know. I had to burn it. And when I did, it was like pulling off a heavy, itchy wool sweater."

Peanut Butter stood on Bea's lap and pushed her head into my arm.

Just then, we both heard the door downstairs open and Aunt Astrid call for us.

"We're upstairs!" we both yelled in unison.

"Bea! Thank goodness you're okay. Good call, Cath." She rushed to hug the both of us. "I noticed before I came over here that something had been chewing on the protection spell at your house, Cath. And my goodness, Bea, they nearly punched a hole right through yours."

"Figures they're after you," I said. "You always did have the looks in the family."

"Yeah, you're the one the boys found so mysterious like a rebel," Bea teased back.

I laughed. I had been on a few dates here and there, but whether it was because I was rebellious or mysterious or just too hard to please, the majority of those never resulted in more than two dates.

I found it hard to be interested in a guy who found so much pleasure in drinking beer or watching sports or both. I just hoped for a bit more. Because I did have these standards, I really didn't date too much.

"You think that is why those little things were creeping outside my window?" I asked.

"No, Cath. Were they really?" Aunt Astrid asked.

"Sure were. Ugly things, staring in at me. But I called their bluff and wouldn't let them in. It was the sage. They must be filthy little monsters, because the smoke cleared them and their depression spell or whatever it was right out of my house."

"If that is what they're doing to the people around here who are killing themselves, my heart just breaks for them," Bea said.

"I don't think they're able to do it to everyone," Aunt Astrid replied, once again taking on that faraway look. "They didn't get a hold of Min or his mom. And Cath, you seemed to be able to rationalize your way through whatever it was they were trying to do. But Bea, you didn't handle it well."

"What about you, Mom? How did you keep them out?"

"I don't know. I felt them and the sad thoughts worming their way into my head, but I can see so many layers of dimensions that I couldn't help but see what they were saying was lies. They were more like pesky, spoiled children not getting their way than anything so dangerous as they were to you."

After a little more talk and a phone call to Jake, letting him know to stop and check on Bea after we had left, we all repeated our tasks regarding the creepy house and made our plan to go back to Prestwick as soon as we were armed.

Plysberger

It took a couple of days, but I finally got a hold of the real estate agent who was supposed to be showing the house off Butternut Drive.

"Good morning. Chelsea Plysberger," said an older, pleasant voice over the phone.

"Good morning, Chelsea," I said cheerily. "My name is Cath Greenstone, and I'm interested in seeing one of the homes that lists your number on the sign."

"How wonderful!" Chelsea said enthusiastically. "Wonder Falls is a lovely place to live. What address are you interested in, Miss Greenstone?"

"I'd love to see 3494 Butternut. That cobblestone driveway is amazing."

For several seconds, I didn't hear anything on the other end of the line except the shuffling of papers.

Finally, Chelsea Plysberger cleared her throat. "When did you want to see the home?" Her bubbly nature was suddenly gone.

"Well, the sooner the better."

"It's a very large home. Do you have a family?"

"I do," I said, getting annoyed. "A big one."

"Um, I think I should tell you 3494 is also a bit of a fixer-upper. Do you have an interest in a house that needs a little TLC?"

"Oh, we assumed as much. Yup, got a plan in place already."

Chelsea gave no reply back.

I continued to talk. "You know how flipping houses is all the rage, right?"

"Do you really think that's such a good idea with such a big place?"

Now I was just getting angry. It was none of her business if I wanted the house to rebuild or to live in as is, whether by myself or with all the Greenstones, still living and even some of those who were not.

"Well, since it's off the beaten path, I'll only be able... that is, there isn't much time and..." She shuffled more papers and cleared her throat.

"I was hoping this afternoon that maybe—"

"No. Not in the afternoon. No, I'm sorry." She chuckled nervously. "Um, I can give you the keys to look around Friday morning. That's my only opening."

"That would be fine and—"

"I'll meet you at the residence at, say, seven a.m."

"Can we make it six thirty? I have to be at work by eight."

"All the better. I'll see you there at six thirty a.m. on Friday, Miss Greenstone."

Chelsea Plysberger hung up quickly, and I sat back and scratched my head. Either she was the worst real estate agent in the world, or she didn't want anything to do with that particular house. I took it as the latter. I wondered what she knew that we didn't.

Later at the café, I told my family we had an appointment to go back and told them about my exchange with Miss Plysberger.

"That leaves us just barely enough time to prepare ourselves," my aunt said. "But I have a gut feeling we're in for a bumpy ride even if we had a month to prepare."

"Then maybe we should take a month," Bea said with a shaky voice, smiling through her nervousness.

"Did Jake tell you anything more about Eshelman or anyone else for that matter?"

"Not really. No. He let me look at his file, but the guy didn't say anything too unusual. I mean, he was off his medication and didn't seem to remember too much about the house. Or if he did, he wasn't saying." Bea ran her hand over her head, pulling her red hair back behind her. "He was mostly just apologizing for what he'd done in the past to Mrs. Roy and expressing his condolences about Mr. Roy. But he was ready to move on. He didn't leave us much to go on."

I hitched up my jeans as if I were John Wayne. "I guess we'll just have to see the place for ourselves."

To tell the truth, I wasn't exactly looking forward to this adventure. At first, I thought bringing the fight to them was the best idea. But after a little thought and a couple of bad visions, well, I was scared, black-eyed kids aside.

Everything about the situation felt backward. Monsters were disguised as children. That was unnerving enough. But then they were residing in a home that was in the most expensive part of Wonder Falls, yet the real estate agent said it was a fixer-upper.

Prestwick was known for having more than one

neighborly dispute over a person who had let their grass grow too long or another who had planted a tree on the wrong two inches of the property line. Yet they had allowed this house to fall into disarray and didn't seem interested in calling out the unknown owner. That was a peculiarity in itself.

Bea had hoped she might be able to get into the hospital to talk to Mr. Krueger, who had tried to hang himself, and maybe help him feel better while picking his brain. Unfortunately, he had died as a result of his injuries.

Aunt Astrid spent the next few days researching concealment spells and digging up talismans for us to carry. She also stepped into the potion business and made a brew for us to drink before we went on our journey.

"What's in it?" I asked, smelling the dark liquid.

"Oh, you know. The usual. Eye of newt, tongue of frog, just a dash of spider web, a pinch of snake venom."

Both Bea and I chuckled.

"Actually, it's just got some green tea leaves, a pinch of arrowroot, and a few special flowers from Romania that have an enchantment all their own."

"Oh, yeah? What do they do?" I asked.

"Well, to put it simply, they should make us

invisible. It isn't for long, but it might be just enough time to get in and get out."

My eyes widened. "Wait. Are you serious? We'll be totally invisible."

"No. Not totally. Remember that movie with the thing in the trees hunting those people in the jungle, and it reflected the light around itself to give the illusion of being invisible? That's what we're doing, except it's more on a fifth vibration level instead of our normal planet-Earth, three-dimensional level. Get it?"

I looked at Bea, who was nodding her head in agreement.

I looked back at my aunt. "You may as well be speaking in calculus, Aunt Astrid. I'll just take your word for it."

We also brought our felines to the house for added strength. Treacle had a sense that something strange was going on at the house but had been at Old Murray's animal shelter being pampered and fed for the past twenty-four hours.

After I had seen those black-eyed children peering in my house, I was worried about him. But before I could call out to him telepathically, he was calling me. I told him to stay where he was until I knew it was safe. He knew exactly where to slink off to.

Now that all six of us were together at Aunt Astrid's house, it was time to do what we had planned. The sun had yet to come up, but the sky was a beautiful gray with pink undertones. The wind had picked up, making the thinning tree branches wave their bony fingers a little to tug off any remaining leaves.

Halloween was just around the corner, and people were decorating for the season. Some embraced fall with pumpkins, scarecrows, bales of hay, colorful gourds, and corn. Others went in the opposite direction with zombies crawling out of their flowerbeds and bloody ghosts hanging from trees.

The more gruesome decorations didn't bother me like they did some people. I knew regular people liked to be scared. The problem with being a witch was that I knew the things lurking in shadows were far worse than any rubber mask, but I couldn't say anything to anyone. Like now. Sure, I could tell my aunt or I could confess to Bea that I was terrified to go to that house. And they would totally understand as they took my hand, and we went together.

Just once, I would like someone to say *don't go* or *I don't want you to go. I'm afraid you'll get hurt*. I'm sure

I would go anyway, but it sure would be nice to hear someone say they were worried about me as much as I was worried about myself.

"Okay, ladies. Are we ready?" Aunt Astrid asked.

I looked at the coffee mugs on the counter. Each one was different. I took the one in the shape of a black cat, his tail forming the handle. I smiled as I looked at my feline, who jumped up on the counter and head-butted me some affection.

But that went away quickly when I took a whiff of the dark concoction inside of my mug. "Oh, this doesn't smell good at all."

"Well, you aren't supposed to bathe in it," my aunt replied. "You're supposed to drink it."

"Gosh, Mom. I'm with Cath on this. I don't know if I can choke this down."

"Fine." Aunt Astrid raised her mug. The words *Head Witch in Charge* were written across it in cute lettering, above which was a svelte witch with big cat eyes riding her broom. "You girls don't have to drink it. We'll just go on over to that house and take a peek like we did yesterday and..."

As if we were two children who had been told Santa wouldn't come unless we ate our vegetables, Bea and I threw back the smelly liquid, gagging and choking after we swallowed it down.

"Yikes." Bea hacked. "That was horrible. Anything that tastes that bad has to be powerful."

"I think it was foot-flavored," I said.

Aunt Astrid drank hers just as quickly but didn't complain nearly as much.

"Now, you each need to put these on." Aunt Astrid handed Bea a brooch made of dried wild-flowers and small seed pods with a sterling silver swirly symbol on a mother-of-pearl base. She quickly pinned it to her shirt.

She gave me a necklace with an opaque black stone that looked like an onyx in the center, surrounded by a plain silver frame.

My aunt also had on a necklace that contained a large silver ball with etched swirls on it. I could hear it jingle slightly when she moved. There was something inside it, but I wasn't sure what.

"Okay, girls. Clasp hands. One last thing."

We did as we were told with our cats each at our sides as my aunt called to the four winds, to the elements of fire, water and earth, to the spirits of the trees, and our spirit guides from the other dimensions to come to our aid and protect us as we went on our journey to cause no harm and in turn, to not be harmed.

We repeated her words. Then we each made a

promise to the universe to leave things as we found them without disruption, corruption, or pollution. In return, we asked for the blanket of protection to allow us to pass easily from the Butternut house back home again.

I had never heard this incantation before. But when we were finished, I felt the universe had accepted our terms and was going to allow us a safe passage. This was, after all, just a trip to look around. No harm in looking.

It all sounded good on paper.

Fleur-de-Lis

❦

"I hope we didn't miss her," Bea said as she pulled into the cobblestone driveway. "It's only 6:37, and I don't see her anywhere. She wouldn't leave after seven minutes, right?"

"Maybe she's up by the gate," I suggested, pointing ahead of us.

Bea nodded and drove up to the wrought iron fence, but there was no one there. She parked the car, and we all sat there quietly, looking around.

Within seconds of our arrival, a set of screeching tires and a loud honking horn tore up the driveway behind us.

"That must be her," Aunt Astrid said.

We all turned to see a spotless white Cadillac come to a jerky halt. Without shutting off the engine, a woman as polished as her car climbed out.

"I'll go talk to her." I quickly climbed out of the back seat.

"Hello." I extended my hand to shake. "You're Chelsea, right?"

Chelsea Plysberger was about my aunt's age but at the other end of the style spectrum. She wore a very expensive tan pantsuit, her nails were impeccably manicured, her hair was a perfect shade of blond, and she wore a lot of makeup. Her lipstick indeed matched her fingernails. She smelled of a spicy perfume that was quite pleasant, and had we met under different circumstances, I would have enjoyed talking to Chelsea Plysberger.

"Yes. You must be Miss Greenstone. I must apologize, Miss Greenstone. I have somehow overbooked my schedule."

She was rattling off her words at record speed, and I could barely keep up. Before I knew it, she was shaking my hand good-bye, handing me a key, practically jumping behind the wheel of her car, and backing out of the long driveway in what could have only been described as an almost hysterical manner.

"What in the world was that?" Aunt Astrid asked, climbing out of the passenger side of the car.

"Okay. We have the keys to unlock the gate and the front door." I shrugged. "Mrs. Plysberger had double-booked her schedule and forgot she had a closing she absolutely had to be at and in fact was already late to. She said to leave the keys in the mailbox at the end of the driveway when we're done."

My aunt and cousin were as shocked as I was.

"I don't think she likes this house," I said.

Bea and my aunt got back in the car as I unlocked the wrought iron gate. Flecks of orange rust came off on my hands. The heavy chains clanked loudly as I unwound them from the bars and set them off to the side along with the padlock.

The gates screamed out a rusty croak as I pulled them open, indicating they hadn't been opened in quite some time.

Waving Bea through, I climbed back into the backseat of the car.

"Okay. Here we go," she said, slowly driving.

From where we were, we couldn't see the house. We drove a good distance along the winding cobblestone driveway and over a quaint wooden bridge that thankfully looked in good enough condition to support the weight of Bea's Chrysler.

"The cobblestone on this driveway alone had to cost a small fortune," Aunt Astrid mumbled.

"I had that exact same thought myself," I said.

Finally, we saw the house. It wasn't at all what I had expected.

"I don't know about you guys, but I was expecting a castle with a moat or something and Christopher Lee, peering out at us as lightning flashed across the sky," I said.

Bea chimed in. "Me too."

"I'm surprised," Aunt Astrid said pensively.

The house had a circle driveway, allowing us to easily turn around and head back the way we had come. In the middle of the circle was a beautiful fountain. It wasn't working and had grown dingy from neglect. It featured a majestic lion head and the fleur-de-lis design at the top.

But it was the house that was truly breathtaking.

It was all white with four pillars across the front. Large floor-to-ceiling windows flanked each side of the massive dark wooden front door. The second-floor balcony stretched the entire length of the front of the house, and four sets of floor-to-ceiling windows divided it up.

"It's pretty," Bea said.

"Jeez, it sure is." I shook my head in disbelief. "And Mr. Eshelman had to think he was the luckiest guy in the world to get this whole place for six hundred per month. My gosh, you'd be stupid not to move right in."

We both waited for Aunt Astrid to chime in, but she didn't. She was studying the architecture as if she were looking for something. And indeed she was.

"There." She pointed up to the middle peak of the house. Etched in the molding was the image of an octopus. It was barely visible unless I was looking for it. "That shouldn't be there. Not if this were just an ordinary house."

We walked up to the grand door. It was made of dark, thick, beautifully distressed wood that would be impossible to kick open. The knocker was also the image of an octopus.

"Seems to be a reoccurring theme." I pointed to the brass design. "What exactly does it mean? I mean, we know little black-eyed children didn't build this place. So who did?"

"Yeah, and what were they trying to do?" Bea asked.

"It's funny you girls ask. The records about this house drop off after the last two owners. Both of those people bought the place sight unseen. All the transactions were done electronically. It's a very mysterious thing. Elroy Nabiski is currently paying the property taxes. He is a lifelong resident of Palm Beach, Florida."

"What connection does he have here in Wonder Falls?" I asked.

"I don't know," my aunt said. "When I tried to get a hold of him to ask him about the property—I mean, it is for sale, right?—he never returned my calls. You'd think someone trying to unload this piece of land for as long as he has would be jumping at the phone if they knew it was a perspective buyer."

"That is odd." Bea looked around the property. "Look. Another octopus." She pointed to the fountain I had admired when we'd first pulled up. I hadn't even realized it, but octopuses were entwined all along the border of the design.

I didn't say anything else but looked at the keys in my hand. "You guys ready?"

They nodded.

Stepping up the cobblestone to the front stoop, I went to unlock the door. My hands were shaking just a little. "Aunt Astrid, I'm afraid your potion might be wearing off on me."

"It wasn't a potion to remove fear, honey," my

aunt said. "It was a potion to enhance courage. Being afraid isn't a weakness. It's an alarm system. One that is very important."

Nodding, I turned the key, heard the giant click, and turned the knob. With the help of my shoulder, I leaned against the door and pushed it open. It groaned like the gate had, and some spiders were disturbed as their webs were destroyed.

We all peeked our heads in. A collective sigh escaped us.

I don't know what we expected to find as we looked into the grand foyer. I knew in my mind, I wouldn't have been surprised to see headless bodies or bloody entrails all over the floor. But we all shook our heads in shock at the beauty and brightness of the room. Beautiful mosaic tiles covered the floor, and the stark white walls were accented with dark wood crown molding. The stained glass designs on the windows gently fractured the light, leaving pretty designs on the walls and floor. On a sunny day, they would probably be prisms.

"So, should we check out the whole house or just look for the heart?" I asked. My voice bounced back to me from the open, empty room.

"I'd really like to explore this place," Bea said. "I'm just so surprised at how beautiful it is."

"I am too. But no, Cath is right. We need to find what we came here for and then get out quick." Aunt Astrid pulled a small dowsing rod from the side pocket of her skirt, held it up, closed her eyes, and whispered. Neither Bea nor I could hear what she was saying, but the rod lowered itself and began to pull her.

Her eyes remained closed, yet she was sure of every step she took. She had no hesitation at all. She saw alternative dimensions and time periods at the same time when her eyes were open. I could only imagine what she could see when her eyes were closed.

We followed her through what probably used to be some kind of receiving room. Past that, toward the back of the house, was a family room. The same floor-to-ceiling windows looked out onto a back patio that showcased a vast array of beautiful trees. Even though they were void of all their leaves, they looked majestic and noble.

"Those would make perfect climbing trees," I said. No one answered me.

I followed behind my aunt and cousin as the divining rod continued pulling us all toward what looked like a pantry. It stopped pulling there.

My aunt opened her eyes.

"This is the heart?" I asked, looking around the small room. "The gallbladder, maybe. Appendix? Possibly. But I wouldn't call this the heart."

Bea pointed to the wall opposite us. "What is that?"

"That's called a wall, honey." I bumped her with my hip. "This is like a pantry, except the kitchen is on the completely other side of the house. This doesn't make sense."

"I see it, Bea." Aunt Astrid took a few steps forward and put her hands against the wall. As she pushed hard, we all heard the click. And there it was.

"A secret passage? No way." I was shocked. "Good eye, Busy Bea."

It popped open, and we looked inside. I felt Bea's hand in mine and was glad she took it.

"That smells like your mom's potion tasted," I whispered to Bea, who nodded.

"This is the heart. And it is black." The words from my aunt did not sit well with me.

I wasn't sure if it was the potion or my own will, but I followed behind her as she stepped into the darkness. Again proving she was prepared for just about everything, my aunt pulled a flashlight from her pocket. When she switched it on, we saw stairs that led down.

"Of course," I grumbled. "Because we can't have the heart of the house just be a walk-in closet on the second floor or even maybe a powder room in the main living room. Nope, it's got to be way down deep in the dirt and dark underneath the house."

"Be thankful it's cemented," Bea said, squeezing my hand.

"Yeah, I guess." I listened intently, trying to hear if anyone was coming up behind us. The door we had just passed through stood open with daylight coming in. I took a couple more steps and looked back, expecting to see some terrifyingly deformed creature or a half-man half-mutant standing at the top of the stairs, glaring at us. But even in this weird crawl-space, if I listened hard enough, I could hear the birds singing outside.

We continued with my aunt leading the way. I brushed my hands across the wall as we carefully went down the stairs, and I felt something familiar. A light switch. I flipped it on, and the greenish glow of an overhead fluorescent light brought an eerie illumination to the stairs.

Both my cousin and my aunt jumped as they turned around to find me with my hand still on the switch.

"Sorry. Didn't mean to scare you." I looked up at the ceiling and around at the walls.

"Well, I can't say I'm not glad you found that," my aunt said as we continued to inch our way further and further down.

"How far down do these steps go?" Bea wondered out loud.

They wound around and around in a spiral until finally, we saw the bottom. I almost wished we had given up before then and headed back up.

At the bottom of the stairs was just a plain cement floor. There were no windows, no water heater, or boiler, or furnace, or fuse box like other basements had. That was because we were not in the basement. We were in the heart of the house. And right smack in the middle of the heart was a grotesque hole that also led down.

"Don't get too close to the edge," I warned. "Aunt Astrid, what is that?" I pointed to the gaping maw in the ground. It looked sickly, if a hole in the ground could look sickly. But to me, it did. A crusty-looking gunk around the edges of the hole looked like spoiled cottage cheese. Where that spread out, there was black, wet-looking mossy stuff growing from it.

The hole in the center was a darker black than I had ever seen in my life, as if I were looking into outer space, devoid of stars. The deepness and vastness of that darkness was almost as dark as this well or pit in the root cellar of the house.

"That's where it's coming from," my aunt said, cringing. She stood back against the wall, studying the room and whatever else it was that she saw.

"It? What *it*? I thought it was *them*. You remember? The black-eyed kids? *Them*?"

"Yes, I remember, Cath. But *it* is what lets those creatures in and out, a gatekeeper of sorts. And it is in there."

"So what do we do now?" Bea asked, inching her way closer to the hole.

"Maybe I'm being paranoid, but Bea, could you please not get any closer to the edge?" I asked. "Bea?"

She either didn't hear me or just ignored me because she stood with one foot almost at the lip of the hole and the other planted behind her.

"Come on, Bea."

Ignoring me, she leaned over and looked in.

That was when the screaming started.

The Well

❦

"Oh my God! Jake! No! It's Jake! He's down there!" Bea's eyes were three times their normal size as she stared into the hole and then at me. "You've got to help me!"

Looking at my aunt, I saw she was confused and terrified all at once.

I took two quick steps toward Bea but stopped short. It didn't make sense. Why would Jake be down there? He had no reason to even come to this house. And how could he have gotten in when the place was locked up tight from the outside?

"Bea, give me your hand," I said. She was near hysterics, and I was afraid she would lose her balance.

I inched my way closer to her and peered as best I

could down into the darkness. Even if Jake had wanted to go down there, he couldn't. There was no ledge, no ladder, no rope, nothing to hold on to. He would have had to be floating.

"He's slipping! Cath! He's slipping!"

"Bea, he's not down there. Nothing is down there." I kept my cool on the outside even though my heart was pounding so hard, I could feel my pulse in my feet.

My aunt was not moving from her spot against the wall. I couldn't tell what she was doing, but I felt that if I didn't grab for Bea, she was going to dive headfirst into that nothingness, and I'd lose her forever.

"He can't hold on much longer! He's going to fall!" she screamed in my face.

I didn't know what was scarier—the house, the darkness, or the madness in Bea's eyes.

"Jake's not here!" I yelled firmly, grabbing her arm.

It was impossible to pull her back. She yanked away from me and got down on her hands and knees ready to lower herself down into that hole, reaching for something she was seeing that I knew wasn't her husband.

"He's barely holding on, and you won't even help

him!" She sobbed. "Jake! Jake!" She lowered one leg over the side.

I got on my belly and grabbed hold of her arm. "He's not there, Bea! Nothing is there! Trust me!"

She shook me off, and in my head, I was sure I saw her tumble into that giant, mouth-like hole and disappear with a scream. But just as I tried to grab her again, her mother stepped in.

Walking bravely up to Bea, she took hold of her daughter's arm and with one yank, pulled her up and away from the opening. Then came the thunderous voice I hadn't heard since I was a kid.

"Beatrice Louise Greenstone!"

She was in such a fury that I was afraid my aunt was going to push Bea right down into that hole. But she didn't. She grabbed Bea like an ornery child having a fit in a department store, and yanked her to her feet with strength I didn't know she had. Bea looked at her mother in shock and anger, and when she began to scream and cry, my aunt slapped her so hard across the face that *my* teeth chattered.

"He isn't down there, Bea!" she yelled.

Bea looked shocked. In all our life together, I had never seen her mother lift so much as a finger toward her or me. And quite frankly, we were too scared to do anything to cross her anyway. Maybe it wasn't really being scared, but we respected her so much we just didn't want to disappoint her by acting bad. I'm not sure. But at that moment, I watched Bea's eyes fill with tears of pain and confusion.

"He isn't down there, honey." My aunt touched her child's cheek gently. "He isn't."

Maybe Bea began to cry really hard. I couldn't tell because I was crying.

"Let's get out of here," Aunt Astrid said coolly. "I know what needs to be done." She pulled Bea with one hand and grabbed a hold of me with the other, leading us back up the stairs as though we were ten years old again.

But as we climbed each step, I heard something behind us. It wasn't my imagination or an echo of our footsteps. It sounded wet and squishy, reminding me of the sound a can of condensed soup made when I shook it out of a can. Something was slithering up out of that pit. Before we disappeared around the corner of the winding staircase, I looked behind us and saw them. Thick tentacles that were a sickly looking gray color were oozing out of that darkness, searching blindly for our heels.

Aunt Astrid pulled us quickly along and out of the room then slammed the hidden door shut before the thing reached the top of the stairs. If she knew it was creeping up behind us, she didn't say anything. I listened but heard a silence more unnerving than the slithery sound of those horrible tentacles.

With all of the protection we came in with, the creature had still gotten a hold of Bea. Had it known about Jake? Had it known she had helped heal him? Was this a personal attack, or were we all in for it?

As we made our way back through the house, I looked out the windows to the backyard. Part of me expected to see our little black-eyed friends out there peeking in. But I didn't. I only wished it would have been them.

I didn't know how long we were down there. It seemed like only a couple of minutes. In that time, the sun had pushed its way through the clouds. The bright oranges and yellows of the fallen leaves made a pretty fall blanket across the ground. I almost didn't see Treacle hanging by his neck from the tree closest to the house at the edge of the patio.

"Wha..." was all I choked out.

I swallowed hard. Unable to look away, I realized that Marshmallow and Peanut Butter were also strung up there. They had all been beaten. Tortured.

Starlight Elixir

I didn't realize my feet had stopped moving. Standing stone still at the window, I felt a wave of sadness and guilt rush over me. Dare I look at the swinging thing to my right?

It was a man. I knew it was. Without looking directly at it, I knew who it was. But I couldn't bring myself to look. No. It wasn't real, and I knew that. But even though I knew it was all in my head, if I looked and saw who it was, it would be burned into my mind. There was no telling how long the image would stay there. It was bad enough I was going to see Treacle, my beloved pet, in nightmares about this day. I couldn't bear the idea of a person in my life being dreamt of in that way.

"Cath!" That voice. It sounded far off.

"Come on, Cath, honey! It's time to go!"

I nodded and followed my aunt. I didn't look back out into the yard. I focused on Bea, who was pale and trembling.

As I crossed the mosaic-tiled floor, I realized the image the tiles made was also an octopus. Had I gone upstairs and looked down from the landing, I would have seen the perfect image of the monstrous beast all at once. As it was, I saw just the tentacles as I hurried my pace, fearful they might come to life and drag me down into that darkness.

Outside, the air felt good and cold. Bea began to cry. I nodded at my aunt then felt in Bea's pocket to grab her car keys. I dashed to her Chrysler and got the engine roaring.

"I saw him in there, Mom," Bea cried. "I saw him."

"No. You didn't, Bea." Aunt Astrid looked at me. "Can you drive?"

I nodded as they piled into the back seat. As soon as the door slammed shut, I sped around the circle, tore out down the cobblestone drive, and didn't slow down until we were in front of the Brew-Ha-Ha. The ride felt as if it had only taken seconds.

My mind hadn't registered any stop signs or green lights. It was as if I were driving in my sleep.

When the sight of familiar landmarks snapped me out of it, I couldn't believe how far we had traveled. And the weird thing was that I didn't get lost coming out of Prestwick. My autopilot seemed to know where to go while I momentarily checked out.

I parked the car and let out a deep sigh. My body began to ache, and my head was beginning to feel the pressure of magic burnout. I couldn't quite understand it, because it was Aunt Astrid's potion and spell that we had used. We didn't do battle or have so much as harsh words for any entity. I couldn't figure out why we were so drained.

"That is what it does, girl," Aunt Astrid said, helping Bea out of the car.

"I'm all right now, Mom." Bea shook her head as if she had also just woken up from a trance or a weird dream. I saw Bea's eyes, and they seemed to look everywhere but at me. She was embarrassed.

After everything we had been through together, this horrible experience was nothing any of us could have foreseen or controlled. She didn't know I had seen something too. She didn't know that I was freaking out on the inside, wondering if what I had seen was just a trick or if it was a premonition. How could I tell her when she felt so bad for nearly throwing herself down a well into oblivion?

Aunt Astrid quickly went to the kitchen, where Kevin was already busy baking. He gave a quiet salutation and went back to his work, as usual, not paying much attention to us. That guy really loved to work in the kitchen.

My aunt returned with two bottles of water and two wet washrags. She handed one of each to us.

"What do you mean when you say that's what it does?" I asked, rubbing my face with the wet rag and cracking open my bottle of water.

"That creature in that pit doesn't just hope for strangers to come and visit the house so it can suck their life forces from them. It reaches out for people. It sends other entities to do its dirty work."

"How do you know this, Mom?"

Sitting down at the counter, Aunt Astrid began to knead her hands. "Because I saw them. There was a whole army of abominations waiting to crawl out of the hole and feed. But you see, they can't all come in at once. They have to take turns, earn their place. But..."

"But? What?" I asked, sipping my water with hands that wouldn't stop shaking.

"But if they accomplish their goal, we may be in for a bigger and longer fight that I'm not so sure we'll win."

"What does that mean, Mom?"

My aunt shook her head and pursed her lips together. "I can't say just yet." Both Bea and I could tell she was hiding something. "Can you two manage the café without me today? I need to do a little digging, and it will probably take me most of the day, if not all of the remaining sunlight to find what I'm looking for."

Bea and I nodded. It wasn't that we didn't like working with Aunt Astrid. She was great, and we loved all being together. But she was the boss. There was something wonderfully playful about coming to work and having the boss gone for the day. It was like a snow day in the middle of fall. We were almost instantly transformed back into teenagers.

"We'll be all right, won't we, Bea?"

"Sure. I'm feeling much better already," Bea said. "But I would like to call Jake, just to be on the safe side. Just to know he's all right."

I nodded and motioned to the café phone.

"All right," Aunt Astrid said. "Are you sure you're both doing okay? Does anyone need a Starlight Elixir?"

"Ugh! Gross!" Bea said. I held my stomach and shook my head sternly back and forth.

Just the thought of a Starlight Elixir was enough

to make me throw up. That was what it did. The name wasn't fooling anyone. Sure, it sounded all pretty and soothing until I tried to choke it down. Then every toxin, every germ, every bad vibe, dirty look, negative thought, or magical residue that had ever accumulated in my system from my toes to the top of my head came rushing out of me. And the elixir couldn't even promise that I would throw up. Things might decide to go south, and that was just as bad.

"Well, when this is all over, we might all be smart to suffer the side effects and toast to our health," Aunt Astrid said as she left the café.

I put my hand on Bea's shoulder and pretended to heave. "You don't think she'll make us do that, do you?"

"If I know my mother, you better just get ready to say ahh."

"Turn to the right and cough?" I joked, making Bea giggle.

We talked and laughed a bit throughout the day. But unlike other times when we had been left to mind the store, there was a cloud hanging over both of us. I couldn't speak for Bea, but I just wanted to ignore it. I didn't want to talk about what I had seen or what Bea had done. I wanted to forget it all. I never thought I'd ever back down from a fight, but this one, those black-eyed kids and their multi-armed pet in the pit were too much. I was scared, more scared than I had ever been before. I wasn't even sure why. I mean, we had gone up against ghoulies and ghosties and demons before, but there was something about this that had needled its way into my head and was not budging.

"What are you thinking?" Bea asked, bumping me with her hip as the evening started to darken the sky outside.

Thankfully, it was a slow night, and there were only two people in the café. One had earbuds in, and the other seemed to be engrossed in his own thoughts.

"I don't know." I took a deep breath. "Something is... not right. Did you ever get that feeling that something is going to happen?"

"Like a storm or something?" Bea asked, fluttering her long eyelashes as if she were trying to hold back a sudden burst of tears while she stacked the cups underneath the counter for the next morning.

"Yeah. A storm." I looked at her then out the big glass window of the café.

"Are you scared, Cath?"

"More scared than I should be. I've got this feeling like something is watching me walk along the edge of a cliff and just waiting for the right moment to jump right out and scare me so I fall."

"It would look like you jumped."

"What?"

Bea pushed her pretty red hair away from her face. "If you were walking along a ledge like on Route 66 where that big drop-off is and someone scared you, it would look like you jumped when in reality, someone else caused you to fall."

"That's exactly right. You feeling it too?"

"Yes." She stretched and squared her shoulders. "But Jake is at the station, safe and sound, and Blake is with him. They'll watch out for each other. Sort of like you and I do." She smiled broadly, and I couldn't resist smiling back.

I walked up to her behind the counter and took her hand. "There is no one on the planet I'd rather be scared to death with than you."

"Yeah, right." She gave me a huge, knowing grin while squeezing my hand.

"What? Who? Who would I rather be scared to death with than you? Tell me. Because I have no idea what you're alluding to. No idea at all."

Her laugh was loud and contagious, and I

played as dumb as I possibly could, but I had the feeling that Bea was talking about Detective Samberg. I tried not to smile but felt my cheeks ignite with embarrassment. I might as well have confirmed her suspicion in writing. But I said nothing and went about cleaning the tables off until I froze in my tracks and pointed out the window.

"What is it?" Bea asked, walking up behind me.

Two children were standing across the street, staring at the café. More likely, they were staring at us.

"What do you think they're doing?" Bea walked up next to me and folded her arms in front of her as if daring them to try to step foot in our café.

"I think they're watching us. Do you get the feeling they're mad?"

"Yup. I think they're mad they missed us at the house. I think they're mad we got out of there and aren't contemplating suicide." She looked at me seriously. "You're not thinking of suicide, are you? Oh, please be honest. You know I'll help you fix it if you—"

"No." I looked at Bea as if she had lobsters coming out of her ears. "I'm certainly not thinking of killing myself."

"I just wasn't sure, you know, with Detective Samberg working so many hours and—"

"Would you please give that up?"

We both looked out the window to see the children had gone. *Poof.* Just vanished into thin air.

"Where'd they go?" I shouted, more to myself than anyone else. I went to the door, but before I could burst through to look up and down the sidewalks, Bea grabbed my hand.

"Wait! That might be just what they want, to get you to open the door or step outside."

I froze in my tracks. "Those sneaky little brats."

"Aren't they, though?" Bea narrowed her eyes and scanned the sidewalk from the door.

We stood in silence for a few minutes until both customers, probably wondering what we were mumbling about, decided it was time for them to go.

"Thank you and have a good night," I said as I handed the earbud guy his change.

"Be safe," Bea added. "Don't talk to strangers on the way home or any weird little kids."

The guy nodded and looked at us as if he suspected we had both been drinking.

"Should we pay your mom a visit before we go home?" I asked.

"Yeah. I think that would be a good idea."

Gloklad

⁂

Aunt Astrid had spent the entire day at her home tearing through her extensive library looking for what, I couldn't quite say. But from the looks of her place, she had done a bang-up job.

Books from the upstairs rooms had been added to the mountains of books already in her living room and kitchen. Old tomes with exotic lettering etched on leather covers were spread open along with contemporary booklets and article clippings. Some books were written in English and some in other languages I didn't dare try to pronounce for fear of conjuring up a dirt devil or vegetable ogre that would wreak havoc on my family.

"Hey!" I had shouted as we'd let ourselves in the

front door. "Must be nice to just take the day off." I walked up and kissed my aunt on the cheek. "Right, Bea?"

"Oh, yeah," Aunt Astrid said. "My daughter and niece were almost swallowed by a bottomless pit, but I think I'll just curl up with a good book or two today."

Truthfully, my aunt looked as if she had been moving furniture. Her hair was messed up, and she had about four different pencils sticking out from it at all angles. Her sleeves were rolled up, and her feet were covered in her pink, fuzzy, not-going-outside-anymore-today slippers.

Marshmallow was lying on a tall stack of books, and the top one lay open to some random page. Her feet hung off the edges, and her tail bobbed lazily up and down.

"Hey, pretty," I said to her in my head. *"What's been going on?"*

"Well, all I can say is that Mom has been very busy today. When she came home, I thought it was going to be a day of unwinding balls of string and perhaps a sprinkling of catnip." The cat looked at me with a serious face. Her tongue stuck out to lick over her pushed-in nose then retreated back into her mouth. *"There was no fun*

at all except for the different pages I got to sit on all day. That has been fun."

I smiled and petted her gently so as not to disturb the stability of Marshmallow's book perch.

"You girls look a lot more like your old selves," my aunt said, barely looking up at us as she picked up a huge book I'd never seen before.

"What in the world is that?" I asked.

The book was about two feet long and six inches thick. It was so dirty and worn that I could barely make out the lettering and symbol on the front.

"It's the Gloklad," My aunt said, hoisting the mighty thing on top of her dining room table, which was already sufficiently covered with a number of puny books. "So far, it's the only book that has anything remotely like a solution to our black-eyed children infestation and their pet land kraken."

"We saw them." Bea moved some books to the floor and sat on the very edge of Aunt Astrid's cozy loveseat. "They were checking us out at the café. But when we looked away for a second, they were gone."

"I don't know. They're kids," I said. "Maybe all they need is a good spanking and sent to their dimension without any souls. Maybe that will teach them not to be so nasty."

Okay, yes, it was corny, but part of me couldn't help but feel we were being punked by a couple of prepubescent, multi-dimensional juvenile delinquents.

"So, they thought they'd pay us a visit, did they?" Aunt Astrid asked. "I think we've really poked a hornet's nest by going to that house."

"We had to, though. Right?" I asked. "I mean we couldn't just let them continue, could we?"

"Absolutely not." She flipped the big book open and began to run her finger down the columns of descriptions, which were written in the most extreme calligraphy I had ever seen. "Now, what this says is exactly what I thought. Our little visitors are a type of vampire. Except, instead of sucking the blood of the living, they feed on fear—terror to be exact. There is something about that particular human response that they will break through the dimensional barriers to get, especially at this time of year."

"And what about the creature in the basement, secret room thing?" Bea asked, a shiver going through her body.

I would still be shaking if I had been in her shoes. She nearly dove into that thing's lair and looked right into its face, whatever that might look like. Her hallucination could have killed her. I wondered how close one of those tentacles had come to wrapping around Bea's ankle. Now I was the one shivering.

"That is the gatekeeper," Aunt Astrid said. "And whoever built that house originally invited that thing to take up residence there."

"How do you know that?" I asked.

"Because, according to this book, that creature can only become flesh if it is summoned. Otherwise, it drifts through dimensions much like it would if it were a real octopus grasping food as it drifted alone."

"Why would anyone want that thing in their house?" Bea asked.

"When they called on the darker forces for help, that was what answered. People just assumed it would get them what they wanted. But, what so often happens with people blinded by that kind of greed, they didn't realize there would be such a heavy fee. And even suicide won't guarantee the person will be paid in full."

"That makes me mad," I said. "So because of that, we now have to risk our lives to close the door they opened? That hardly seems fair."

"But just think of Mrs. Roy," Bea said. "She lost her husband because of those 'children.' I almost lost Jake to that. Mr. Krueger was just a guy. They almost got Min, and who knows what kind of damage was done to that Shawn Eshelman fellow. He lived there. It was probably only a matter of time before he did something."

My aunt searched through her book until finally she found what she was looking for. "It isn't fair. But we have to stop this. If we don't, then you can bet every year around this time, Wonder Falls will be plagued by a rash of suicides. Those beasts will go unchallenged, and their powers will grow. Then, any hope of ever stopping them might be gone for good."

Bea and I looked at each other. This was serious.

"We need to gather our strength," Aunt Astrid said. "I've found an ensemble of spells that combined, I think, will give us the best chance of defeating this evil. But..."

"Oh, jeez. Of course there's a but," I said. "But what? Do we have to drink blood or cut off all our hair or sacrifice a pinky toe? What?"

My aunt had stopped searching in her book and looked at me with her eyebrows pursed together as if I had just suggested we all soak our feet and heads in a bucket of water at the same time. "The process will take us about three days to prepare."

"Three days?" Bea asked. "What about the café?"

"We'll have to run it in shifts. I'll open, you take

the noon shift, and Cath can close," Aunt Astrid said. "We'll just have to do the best we can."

"Do we need any supplies?" I asked.

"No. I have everything we'll need. I think it would be best if we got started right away."

I really had all the faith in the world in my aunt and her plan. But something inside me tugged hard, and the following words spilled right out of my mouth before I could arrange them tactfully.

"But you put a protection spell on us before and, well, Bea almost did the swan dive into a bottomless pit. And I saw...well, um, I saw it all happen. What makes you think this one will be different? I mean, what if they can see through it and do the same thing?"

The look my aunt gave me was not harsh or hurt. Instead, it was as if she knew something, the same terrible something I had seen but hadn't admitted. I blushed.

"You're right, Cath. That didn't help us too much." Her eyes had a way of letting you know she wasn't just looking at you, but she was seeing half a dozen other things around you. But her smile was just for me. "However, now that I've seen it, I know what it is. And I can tell you, the shift in the astral plain has already begun. I can see its fear in a thousand different ripples in the dimensions. I can sense its anger. And any being that exudes that much negative energy must be scared of something. It can only be us. And that gives us the upper hand."

She went on to explain her plan. Fasting. Chanting. Smudging. There was a whole list of things we each needed to do at certain times of the day and night in addition to running the café as if there was nothing going on.

Not Human

That first day went off without a hitch for everyone except me. When I came into the café to relieve Bea, I found Darla sitting at the counter in my favorite spot where I liked to look out the window and people watch when things were slow.

Bea saw my shoulders slump the minute I saw Darla. She gave me a look that said, "Sorry, but what could I do?"

Pretending I didn't see Darla, I stepped around the counter, grabbed an apron and a rag, and started wiping down the empty tables.

"Hi, Cath." I heard a voice and looked all around to see who said it. "It was me," Darla said meekly, waving at me as if we weren't sworn enemies.

I could have just said hello back and smiled, taking the high road. But I didn't. Instead, I looked at her as if she had just handed me a toad from her purse.

"Can I get you a refill?" I asked, letting annoyance drip from each syllable.

"I was wondering if I could talk to you," Darla said. "It's kind of important."

It was a setup, I was sure. But curiosity killed the cat, and satisfaction brought him back, so I set my dirty rag down next to her designer purse and folded my arms in front of me.

"I know we haven't always seen eye to eye on things, Cath, but..."

Haven't seen eye to eye? I couldn't believe the words coming out of her mouth. This may have sounded harsh to someone who wasn't bullied in high school, but if only those black-eyed children could have found their way to Darla's house, they would have been angels in my book instead of scary little devils who needed to be exorcized.

"...do you think you can introduce him to me?" Darla was asking.

"Introduce who?" I snapped back into this surreal and awkward reality.

"Blake Samberg. He's your cousin's husband's

partner, right? I mean, since Jake Williams is married..."

"Not that *that* has stopped you before." For a moment, I felt horrible those words had tumbled out, but then I didn't.

Her eyes narrowed, and I saw a flash of the old Darla I had known since high school. This was an act. "I was hoping you could introduce me to him."

"Introduce you to Samberg?" I felt myself start to choke. "Why would I do that?"

Darla rolled her eyes as if I had just asked the most unreasonable question ever uttered.

"Because I asked you to? Because I'm an old friend, and we've known each other for years? Maybe that's why?"

I looked over at Bea who was busy untying her apron, looking down. I could tell by her body language that she was trying not to laugh.

"Oh, is that why? Well, let me think for just a minute when I'll see the detective." I picked up my rag and went back to wiping down the tables.

I heard Darla mutter something to Bea. Bea muttered something back, but I didn't turn around until I heard the jingling bells over our front door as it opened and closed.

Whipping around, I snapped my hands to my

hips and looked at Bea. "She's got some nerve," I hissed, watching Bea shake her head in disbelief.

Darla represented a part of my life that Bea was all too familiar with, and she knew full well that unless I had a gun pointed to my head, I wouldn't jump to help Darla out. I especially wouldn't help her sink her fangs into Blake. She wasn't his type at all.

"She definitely asked the wrong person about Blake Samberg," Bea said, quickly stepping around the counter, smirking.

"And what is that supposed to mean?" I asked, my cheeks turning red.

"Good night, cuz. I'll see you this evening at Mom's." And out the door she went without a second look at me.

Thankfully, the afternoon and evening rushes were lighter than usual. It was just a few days before Halloween, and I assumed people just weren't in the mood for coffee or pumpkin spice lattes.

I took out a couple of our paper placemats, turned them over to the blank sides, and began to doodle to help pass the time. Kevin was busy like he always was, whistling while he worked, and keeping to himself as he began to prepare for the next day's menu.

For a second, I thought of going back to talk to him. But the few times I had tried, he'd just smiled happily and gave me yes and no answers to my questions. I got the feeling he may have thought I was lonely so he tolerated my chitchat. The truth was I just didn't want him to think I was rude. Like Jake says, if it ain't broke, don't fix it. So I left Kevin in the back while I drew a picture of Treacle.

As if on cue, I heard the back door open and close. Kevin left it open to keep it cooler back there. The ovens were intense and heated most of the restaurant when the temperatures started to dip. But we didn't mind him leaving the door open for some fresh air.

Treacle slinked his way through the door and hopped up on the counter.

"Where have you been?" I asked, scratching his head.

"Just around. The mice are heading indoors. It's making me mad."

"Well, if you'd come home more often, I'm sure you'll catch some in the garage or in the basement."

He sniffed the air, looking toward the door. *"What is that smell?"*

"Darla was here. Maybe that's the stink you're picking up on."

"No." He began to tense. *"It's not human."*

Before I could ask him another question, he arched his back and hissed at the glass café front door.

There they were. They weren't across the street this time. They were right up against the door, staring in. Two little black-eyed children with plain clothes and pasty skin.

"Let us in," one of them said in a weird voice that sounded more like an echo than the voice of someone right in front of me.

It was like a spider creeping up my spine as I watched the children just staring in at Treacle and me.

"Let us in for eating," the other one said.

The words bounced around in my head like some low-frequency vibration, making the fillings in my mouth throb.

"Cath," Treacle said. *"The back door is open."*

My eyes nearly popped out of my head, and just then I realized I didn't hear Kevin whistling anymore.

Treacle jumped off the counter and stood at the front door. He hissed and growled deep in his gut as if daring them to set foot inside the café. I ran around the counter and burst through the swinging kitchen doors to find Kevin standing at the back door with his arms raised as if in surrender.

"Kevin!" I shouted as I ran and grabbed him by the collar of his T-shirt, yanking him back into the hot kitchen.

"What!" he shouted as he lost his balance and fell backward, reaching for a stack of plates and pots that came tumbling down with a crash.

I didn't look at him until after I had slammed the door shut. "Outside!" I said breathlessly. "The kids!"

"What kids?"

"The black-eyed ki... the kids in the neighborhood."

"What about them?" Kevin asked. "Jeez, I think I broke about ten plates here!"

"Oh, uh, they're coming to the doorways of some of the businesses and throwing eggs."

"Really, Cath? I thought you were taking a grenade explosion for me. Yikes."

"I'm so sorry." I reached down to help Kevin up.

He smiled that same kind smile he always did. "No worries. I've got a good bit of padding." He patted his gut.

"Oh, no. I'm sorry I scared you. Look, it's so

slow. Uh, just let me check the front door, and you can head on home. I'll clean up this mess."

"Are you sure?"

"Yeah, just wait here one minute."

I went to the front of the door and saw Treacle casually licking his paw. *"They are gone,"* Treacle said. *"I don't think they like cats."*

A deep sigh of relief came out of me, and I went back into the kitchen after grabbing my share of tips from the tip jar.

"Here." I handed Kevin the few dollar bills I had gotten. "It's not a lot, but it'll fill your tank with gas. Maybe get you some fast food."

"That's not necessary, Cath."

"No, it is. I guess I just don't know my own strength," I said, trying to chuckle.

"Well, I would have never guessed a tiny thing as pretty as you had that kind of muscle. Remind me not to get on your bad side. But if I ever need a bully put in their place, I know who to call."

This was the most conversation I had ever had with Kevin. I started to laugh as I walked him to the front door. Treacle stepped out of the way as I opened the door.

"See you tomorrow, Cath," Kevin said cheerfully.

"See you tomorrow, Kevin." I locked the door

behind him but waited to make sure he made it to his car, had the lights and engine on, and was pulling away before I went back into the kitchen.

I looked at the broken plates and toppled-over pots and pans. "Thank goodness the stoves weren't on," I muttered. "I could have really gotten him hurt."

"But you didn't," Treacle said. "Just a few broken dishes. I'll help you clean."

Treacle's way of helping me clean was hopping into one of the big stainless steel pots and making himself comfortable as he watched me clean up the broken glass.

After about twenty minutes, I was finished. There were no traces of the chaos that had just taken place, and with the exception of one pot that would need to be washed after my cat had sat in it, everything seemed back to normal.

I locked the café up tight, and with Treacle snuggling happily in my arms, I walked to my Aunt Astrid's house, happy the work day had come to an end.

"You know you're in for a bumpy ride if going home to plan for a paranormal attack sounds like more fun than the day you just had at work." My comment earned me an affectionate head butt from my companion.

The sun had set yet still left an orange glow just above the horizon. The trees, barer today than they had been yesterday, were black, cracked lines that looked like an abstract painting depicting the contrasts between light and dark, color and blackness.

I listened and heard cars driving, the wind blowing, wind chimes echoing from front porches, and my own footsteps.

Somewhere I had read that people automatically started to count their steps when their mind stopped running on all cylinders and for a few seconds, they were just in the moment.

One... two... three... four...

"Do you hear that?" Treacle interrupted as I tried to ignore the world for just a few paces.

Five... six... seven...

"It sounds like something is gnawing on a bone. A really big one."

Eight... nine...

I was at Aunt Astrid's house, barely noticing how quickly I had begun to walk. I stood on her porch, safe within her protection spell. I listened. Yes, I could hear the chewing sound too.

I walked quietly to the edge of the front porch. Peeking around the corner, I saw the same two black-eyed children that were at the café. Scratching and clawing with their hands and biting with their teeth, they appeared to be trying to get past my aunt's protection spell. But when they saw me, they hissed like feral cats and ran off into the darkness.

Psych Ward

❧

For two days, we Greenstone witches had kept up our vigil.

Managing the café in shifts was difficult. With just one of us handling the influx of people morning, noon, and night, and poor Kevin nursing a sore elbow, we appreciated each other all the more.

However, I was learning that sometimes I really just wanted to tell people to shut up and sip their coffee. *Sorry you had to wait five minutes extra to get your tea, and I didn't mean to forget the sprig of lavender. It's just that we're short-handed, and you understand. Well, if you feel you must go to our competitor The Night Owl, then by all means, do that.*

Yeah, right. Where were those black-eyed kids when I needed them?

But Aunt Astrid's home was a plethora of good vibes. As soon as I walked in her door after locking up the café, I could smell the sage and mugwort wafting through the place.

On the stove, in an adorable black kettle, simmered the fragrant spices that were saturating not just the air, but all of us with their magical powers. Sage, of course, chased away evil bugaboos. Mugwort, or sailor's tobacco as it was sometimes called, enhanced the powers of amulets and crystals, which could be seen in the bubbling, boiling water at the bottom of the kettle.

We would each wear one of those. They were not pulled out all the time. Amulets were like glow-in-the-dark stickers. In the right conditions, they would store up power. Then when we needed them, they would glow for a good while, giving off light, energy, a foul smell at the enemy, ear-piercing frequencies only certain spirits could hear, or sometimes a ground-level vibration that drove the enemy mad. But it was temporary. More than one good witch had gotten her lumps because she hadn't prepared her amulet correctly or did it in a hurry.

Aunt Astrid, with Marshmallow at her side, would face out her various windows at certain times of the day, calling in all directions for the powers of nature to help us with our task. It had to be done three days in a row in order for our powers to be strong enough to do battle with those nasties on Butternut Avenue.

It was my turn to address the western skies and spirits in the trees to awaken them from their fall rest and ask for their assistance. I liked incantations, and although they were only used in dire circumstances like ours, I enjoyed the conversation, however one-sided, with these elements of nature.

Speaking with animals was still a blessing, but some of them didn't care to talk back because they probably found my queries to be odd and a little intrusive. But the trees and the wind seemed eager to relate with me, and I felt their strength.

I would keep this up as the moon crossed the sky, and I had to stand at attention for the whole thing. That was hard because I had been on my feet all day. But the spirits appreciated this kind of reverence, and it wasn't a ritual done for comfort. It was done because somewhere, something had upset the balance of our dimension. It wasn't just a lost or misguided entity. It was like a plague of locusts, and if we didn't stop them in the early stages of their infiltration, we might never get a toehold again. Taking a deep breath, calming my mind and pushing out all the stress of the day, I began to recite the passages.

Aunt Astrid was hovering over a bowl of water, with three white candles around her, one on her left, one on her right, and the other directly in front of her. She would also occasionally throw a pinch of salt into the air or sprinkle it over the open flames of the candles, causing them to glow pink or green or even a dark blue.

Everything we were doing had a purpose, and although our rituals may have looked like random actions—shots in the dark to protect us from what we knew we were going to have to face—we knew the strength each was bringing to the fight.

I had started to repeat the words just over a whisper when I heard Jake walk in.

He walked up to Bea and kissed her sweetly on the cheek. "I'm not interrupting anything, am I?" he asked.

"No." She smiled. "We've got a nice assembly line of magic going on here."

"And what is this for, again?" Jake asked innocently.

"Just to chase those black-eyed children from Wonder Falls," Aunt Astrid said. It wasn't a lie. But Jake didn't need to know that we had to take the fight to them. "We're almost finished. Just one more night for the whole thing to be complete."

"And then what?" Jake asked.

"Then we'll have the muscle we need to trap them and send them back to wherever they came from," Aunt Astrid said. "Or at least send them away from here."

"Good," Jake responded. "I'm starting to get a little lonely in the house all by myself." He slipped his arm around Bea and pulled her close to him.

She let out a playful giggle as she elbowed him to a moderately safer distance from her. "How was work today?" she asked.

"Oh, gosh. Well, how was work? Well, it was confusing today, to say the least." Jake quietly pulled up a chair next to the stove where Bea watched the bubbling kettle. Every once in a while, she dropped in another couple of fresh sprigs of sage.

"What happened?" she asked. I leaned in their direction to hear what Jake had to say.

"Well, you remember our friend Shawn Eshelman? The guy who we thought had something to do with the Roys? Well, we had to arrest him."

"What?" Bea gasped. "Why?"

"He had been seen sneaking around the Roy house with an ax."

"What?" Bea's hand flew to her throat.

I turned from the window and looked at Jake.

"What did he have that for?" Bea whispered so as not to totally disrupt my concentration.

"We aren't sure. But he looked like a different person since the last time we saw him. He said he was back at the old place he used to rent and that he wasn't going to hurt anyone. But you don't carry an ax around like some random person might ask you to chop them some wood."

Jake went on to say that the Eshelman kid hadn't bathed for a couple of days. He had obviously been sleeping in the clothes he was wearing, and with the weather getting colder, staying in that drafty, empty house had given him a nagging cough. Had he not had that cough, Mrs. Roy might not have heard him skulking around her house.

"But the weird thing was his eyes," Jake said. "They were half-crazed."

"Was he off his medication again?" Bea asked.

"Yes. The problem now is that he won't be sent to a psych ward. He's got to go to jail, and I'm afraid a guy like him will get worse there before he ever gets better."

"That poor boy," Bea said, shaking her head. "And as if Lisa Roy hasn't been through enough already."

"Yeah." Jake blew out a breath. "Talk about an unlucky streak."

I nodded in agreement but said nothing, paying homage to the setting sun and hibernating trees.

"Yeah, it was a mess," Jake continued. "The Roy family is all in an uproar about it. Eshelman is being held on bond for criminal trespass as well as breaking a restraining order and carrying an ax with intent to cause bodily harm. It took Blake and me hours to get the paperwork started. He told me to come home for a while. He went to check out the house where Eshelman was staying again to see if—"

My blood ran cold. I whipped around in a panic. "What did you say?" My mouth had gone completely dry.

"Cath, wait!" Bea snapped, her own eyes wide with worry. "You have to finish…"

"Blake," Jake said. "He went to that house on Butternut to—"

"Did he go alone?" I snapped.

"Well, probably. Unless he took a uniform, but I doubt it. He likes to do things a certain way without interrup—"

I dropped the book I had been reading from and dashed toward the front door. I reached for the knob just as Aunt Astrid took hold of my hand.

"We can't stop now. We've got to finish what we started." Her voice was kind and soft but firm. I saw the sadness in her eyes as she stood by this awful decision. "We can't help him. Not if we stop."

"We can't just let him go in there! It'll kill him!" I wrenched my hand free, tore open the door, and ran outside. I jumped off the porch and reached my car in what felt like only three or four strides. A moment later, I had the engine roaring to life.

Ask the Devil

I swore I heard my aunt calling after me. It broke my heart what I had just done. All that work and all those hours were for nothing. I had broken the chain and for what? For a guy who probably thought I was a jerk and annoying and stupid.

Just because I had caught him staring at me when he'd come to get his free coffee from Bea, or because he had kept our stakeout a secret from my family, didn't mean he had any feelings toward me other than annoyance.

But I knew what my feelings were toward him. Maybe I couldn't say them out loud. Maybe it was just puppy love, but I couldn't bear the thought of the nasty creatures in that house tormenting him, leaving him feeling hopeless, scratching up his mind like they'd done to Jake.

No. I just needed to get him out of there. And maybe I would beat him to it. Maybe I would get there just as he was pulling in the driveway, and I could talk him out of going inside that God-forsaken structure. Yeah. Sure. He might not even be there yet.

Then I could go back to Aunt Astrid's and apologize, and we could start the whole thing all over. Three more days. Heck, Halloween wasn't for another six days. We had plenty of time.

Right. Okay. As long as Blake hadn't gone into the house yet, I still had a chance to make things right.

But then I was struck with another scare. What if I couldn't find the house again? Prestwick was such a twisty-turny kind of place, and I could get lost like I had before. Plus, it was dark outside, and I wasn't that familiar with the area in the daylight, let alone when all the shadows covered the landmarks and street signs.

"You could ask the devil," I said out loud to myself. The thought made my stomach drop to my toes. I knew Darla could tell me. If I sped up her driveway, I could ask her for the directions just to make sure. But what were the chances she would tell me? After I had basically told her to shove off where Blake Samberg was concerned, she would never help me. In fact, she had probably already been plotting revenge in a dozen different ways, four languages, and two time zones.

"For Blake," I said out loud. "For Blake, I'll stare into the face of the Gorgon."

I hit the gas and tore through town, pulling into the Prestwick neighborhood with a squeal of tires, leaving skid marks on the pavement.

Darla's house was easy to find, and I pulled into her long driveway only to slam on the brakes at the top of the hill.

"Please let her be home," I said as I hopped out of the car, ran to the door, and began pounding away. "That'll be the first and last time I ever say that."

After pushing the doorbell repeatedly and pounding on the door, I finally heard Darla yelling from inside.

"Who the hell is making all that noise?" she yelled in a high-pitched, whiny voice.

"Darla! Darla! It's Cath Greenstone! Open the door!"

"Who?"

"You heard me, Darla! Please! Just open the door!"

For a second, I thought I was going to have to kick it in. With the adrenaline that was pushing me along, I was pretty sure I could have done it. But I was glad I didn't have to find out.

Darla opened the door wearing silk pajamas and a green mud mask on her face. "What do you want?"

"Darla, I'm sorry to bother you so late, but I need your help."

There it was—the grin of a cat that had a mouse wounded and cornered. "Oh, you do? Really? Isn't that funny?"

"Darla, please. I need to know where 3494 Butternut is. I always get lost going through—"

"I don't know where that is," she snapped, making it painfully obvious she knew exactly what I was talking about. Folding her arms over her chest, she glowered at me.

"Darla, a man's life is at stake. Please just help me this one time and…"

"And what? What's in it for me?"

"Oh my God, Darla! What do you want? I just need directions, not a kidney! What is it that you want?"

Her eyes narrowed. "You know." If anyone deserved a punch in the face, I thought it was her.

"Now? You want me to arrange for you to meet Detective Samberg now?" I felt my eyes sting with tears. "Jeez, all right. I'll introduce you to him. Now tell me where that house is!"

She took a step closer to me, put her left hand on the door frame and the other on the open door itself. "No. I just wanted to hear you give in. Now get off my property before I call the cops." *Slam!*

I stood there, trembling with anger and frustration as I stared at the front door she had just shut in my face. I quickly made my way back to my car, fully aware that Darla was watching me through the crack in the curtains, enjoying my tears as she had always done in high school.

I peeled out of her driveway and got back onto the road, heading in the direction I thought was right.

As I tried to calm myself enough to focus, I saw two blinking lights off to the side of the road. Reflectors. A jogger. Maybe that person knew the neighborhood.

Quickly rolling down the window, I pulled up alongside the jogger in the stretch pants. He nearly jumped into the bushes as I stopped the car, his earbuds blocking out the world around him.

"I'm sorry, sir," I said. "Do you know how to get to 3494 Butternut?"

"Sure." He smiled after he realized I wasn't any kind of threat. He told me to take a left and another left and then a right and I'd run right into it. That sounded correct.

"Thanks!" I yelled. I repeated the directions over to myself as I drove away. As I looked in the rearview mirror, I was surprised I didn't see the man. I looked in my side mirror, thinking perhaps he had crossed the street. Nothing. Finally, I turned around in my seat and confirmed there was no man behind me. No jogger.

What the heck was happening? I could have sat there and turned that instance over and over in my head, but I thought I would save it for the next day instead.

"If there is a tomorrow for me," I said, letting out a sad little chuckle. "I'll do like Scarlett O'Hara. I'll think about that tomorrow."

In my headlights, I saw the dilapidated For Sale sign and the cobblestone driveway. Looking at the clock on my dashboard, I saw it had only taken me twenty minutes to get there, including the stop at

Darla's. I still might have made it. I still might have beat Blake there.

But as I sped up, I nearly collided with his car that was parked sideways across the width of the driveway near the gate, which had remained open since Aunt Astrid, Bea, and I had made our quick getaway. There was no squad car, which meant he had most likely come by himself.

"Let him be in the car," I said aloud to myself. I shone my high beams at the car, hoping to see his silhouette in the driver's seat. But it was empty.

Octopus

❦

"**O**f course not!" I yelled to myself. "It can't be easy!"

I threw the car in park and shut off the engine. Holding my breath, I listened for sounds or movement around me. Nothing moved. I got out of the car and heard crickets in the distance. But there was no noise around this house. The reality of what I was about to do sank in. This house, with its open mouth in the basement and wretched visions, was waiting for Shawn Eshelman or anyone else to walk through the door.

"I don't even have Aunt Astrid's protection spell. No sacred amulet. Not even a lucky penny," I grumbled as I looked down the long, dark passage of the driveway. *Should I run or just walk?*

My mind wouldn't hold onto a thought. It just kept jumping from thing to thing.

"Come on, Cath! Think!"

But nothing would come. I couldn't wait any longer and decided that since it had let me in once before, it would either do the same again, or it would try to stop me where I was. When I stepped over the boundary of the fence and was officially on the house property, I began my walk.

By then, it was more than dark outside. The shadows from the trees, shrubs, and sculptures on the grounds seemed to roll and tumble over each other, every section darker than the last. But still, I saw nothing more. No ghostly faces of children looking out at me. Just shadows, keeping the secret of whatever it was they were concealing.

Finally, a mysterious wind kicked up, making the branches and fallen leaves look as if they were now creatures running in the words.

"You just need to get Blake, Cath. Just run in, grab him, and get out. You don't need to fight or stall or anything. Just run in, grab him, and go." I had a few small spells up my sleeve. I knew a distortion spell that could make me appear larger and abstract, like a Picasso, but I didn't think that would help me out too much at the moment.

I also knew how to make the winds blow harder. Perhaps that would help give us some cover once we got out of the house. But what would get me there quickly?

I slapped my head and rolled my eyes.

"Though the wind makes it last, in order and in stable, come to speed and make me fast for as long as I am able."

It was a speed spell I used in high school gym class. Since I'd been a wallflower, no one had ever noticed when I disappeared in one place and showed up a good piece along the racetrack ahead of everyone. And I'd hated gym, so the less work I had to do that made me sweat, the happier I was.

Now I was using this simple little spell to make my way to the house.

Just a few steps, a couple of strides, and I was nearly there.

But as I looked around, I saw something waiting for me or at least waiting for someone to come. Up in one of the higher windows, a figure stood illuminated by a mysterious light. It was just the silhouette, but I felt those black eyes on me. I looked around as I made my way to the front stoop. The door was standing wide open. Behind me, the leaves tumbled over each other, and I was sure something was moving in the woods.

Even though it was a bad habit, I cracked my knuckles when I stopped. Taking a deep breath, I turned my back to the woods and stepped into the house. It was quieter than I had imagined. The door automatically closed behind me. I felt as if I might have just sealed myself into my own tomb. When I tried to pull it open again, it wouldn't budge.

"I'll worry about that once I find him. Now, if I were Blake Samberg, where would I go first?" My heels tapped on the marble floor with each step. "Not to the basement. He'd have no reason to go to the basement. Right? Right. Yes, Cath, you are right. So where do we—"

Thump! Thump!

Looking up the grand staircase, I saw him. Blake looked half-crazed, dragging a huge wooden chair to the landing at the top of the steps. He was crying. And there was a rope hanging down from the light fixture over the stairs to the banister.

"It's got him," I muttered to myself. "He's going to hang himself."

I dashed toward the stairs but then stopped and slowly began to ascend them, one step at a time so as not to freak him out. "Blake! It's me, Cath! Blake!"

He stopped and looked down at me. His face was so sad, my heart broke. I didn't know what it had done to him. What could it have said or shown him that would make his appearance change so much?

"It's me, Blake! Just stop what you're doing and come talk to me." I hoped the desperation didn't come through in my voice.

He looked up at me and smiled a sad smile. "If only it was you." More tears ran down his face as he looked at me. "If only it was you and not those things."

"What things..." I saw them behind him. It was the same two children who had stood outside the café. They were grinning and panting, clenching and unclenching their hands as their black eyes seemed to watch Blake and me at the same time. I felt their evil trying to get into my mind as they stared, but just as I had done before, I concentrated on the space between their eyebrows. I wouldn't fall into that darkness.

But as I took a step, I felt an invisible barrier pushing back. The children were becoming more and more animated the closer I got to them as I walked up the stairs. Then I looked past them down the hallway. I saw the cats, hanging, tortured. Only this time, their legs twitched and kicked with life. My heart broke in pain at the thought of the Greenstone felines, waiting to be saved but help not coming. A shroud of sadness started to collect on my shoulders, weighing me down.

The stairs started to feel like quicksand around my ankles, holding my feet and making them feel as though they weighed a hundred pounds each. I tried to steady myself against the banister, but it moved and swayed like a rope bridge instead of a solid marble staircase.

"It isn't real. Blake!" I screamed at the top of my lungs. "Blake, look at me!"

"You're not real," he said sadly. "I let you die. Before I could tell you how I felt, I let you fall."

"No, Blake." I pushed with all my might against the wall of air that was slowing me down. "Blake, don't do anything else. Just stand there and wait." He looked so handsome in the suit he'd worn to work with a nice, quiet, conservative tie. His shoes were hard-soled, and I didn't think Sam Spade could have looked any cooler than Blake did.

His eyes were red with tears. "If only you were real." He cried as he began to construct the end of the rope into a noose.

I pushed and pushed until finally I had reached the top of the stairs.

"Blake! It's me! I'm really here!" I yelled, tears running down my own cheeks. I saw the happiness and satisfaction in the movements of those demonic children out of the corner of my eyes but didn't take my gaze off Blake. Instead, I took three more staggering steps toward him, pulled my arm back, and roundhoused him across the chin. "Snap out of it!" I screamed.

I then heard a terrifying rumbling from the first level. I knew what it was. Without leaning over the edge of the stair railing, I shifted my eyes to see what I had guessed was on the mosaic-tiled floor when I'd been there with Bea and Aunt Astrid. The octopus.

Gray Flesh

✦

"Cath?"

"Blake! Look out!"

A cloying gray tentacle pulled itself from the tile and wrapped itself around the banister. Then another did the same and another as the beast began to emerge from the design on the floor. It was the same thing I had seen writhing after us down in the basement.

Before Blake knew what I was saying, he was jerked off his feet, landing flat on his back with one of those horrible tentacles wrapped around his ankle. It was trying to pull him over the railing.

Lunging forward, I grabbed his arm, holding on tightly with both of mine. "Hang on, Blake! I've got you!" I hoped I was strong enough to wrestle him out of the kraken's grasp.

"Cath! Help!"

"I've got you, Blake! Just don't let go of me! And don't look over the banister!"

Of course, what does he do but look over the banister.

"What the hell is that?" he screamed, tightening his grip on my hands. "We've got to get out of here, Cath!"

"You'll never leave!" I heard the children hiss from behind me. Both Blake and I looked in the direction of the black-eyed children. They were insane with excitement, as if they were watching a cricket getting slowly digested by a spider. Their breath was coming out in ragged pants, and saliva dripped over their chins. "You'll never make it out alive!"

"Don't look at them, Blake! Don't you dare look at them, or I swear to heaven I won't just punch you! I'll beat the crap out of you! There won't be anything left for that thing to eat! Don't test me!"

Blake stared at me. His hands held fast, and I saw him clench his jaw as his resolve returned.

The tentacle was pulling harder. Then another wormed its way up and also secured itself around

Blake's leg. I swung myself around, holding Blake's arm and bracing myself against the banister, desperately trying to pull him free. But with every tug, it tightened itself, digging deeper into Blake's leg.

"Cath! I can't hold on! You've got to run!"

"What? Are you kidding? I'm not going anywhere without you, Blake! I didn't come all this way so I could let them get you!"

"You came for me?" he asked, his voice strong.

"Well, duh! Do you think I was just passing by this place and thought to stop in?" I tried yanking him back, making him cry out as the pain in his leg started to become unbearable. "Come on, man! Fight!"

Then I remembered something. "Oh my gosh! Blake! Do you have your gun?"

"My what? Oh my gosh! My gun! Yes! Yes!" He let go of one of my hands and tried to reach into his coat to get his firearm from his shoulder holster. That was a lot harder than it would seem considering he was practically upside down.

The two black-eyed children stopped their creepy dance and dove at me, trying to pull me away from Blake since I was only holding one of his hands.

"Ah ha!" he cried triumphantly. Taking careful

aim at the tentacle around his leg, he pulled the trigger.

In an explosion of glistening gray flesh and putrid-smelling ooze, the first tentacle unraveled its wounded self from Blake's leg, dropping him down with a thud.

Quickly sitting up, Blake took aim at the other one still wrapped around his leg. As he went to pull the trigger, the two children jumped on my back, and I felt a searing pain in my spine and on the side of my neck.

The whole room began to spin, and tears flooded my eyes. I tried to cry, but the pain was so bad, it overwhelmed me. All I could do was gasp.

"Get off her, you little freaks!" Blake yelled. He grabbed hold of the beast on my neck and tore him off of me. Instantly, I clamped my hand to my neck and felt the skin burning. There was no blood or open wound, which surprised me because I was sure it had torn my throat open.

There was still a weight on me, but as I tried to turn, I heard Blake screaming. As I looked over my shoulder, I saw him pull his good leg back and then land his foot squarely against the other child-monster that had attached itself to me. The creature flew backward and landed in a disgusting heap of twisted body parts, mangled at unnatural angles. But then, like its companion on the floor below, it twisted and writhed around until it was back on its feet in the shape of a small boy. It wasn't done with us.

"Come on, Cath. On your feet!" Blake slipped his arms underneath mine and yanked me to my feet. The whole room spun, and I leaned into him for support.

He smelled so good. Even after working up a sweat and having gross blood-stuff all over his leg, I thought if his cologne was the last thing I ever inhaled, I would be happy.

The pale children looked at us with hatred in the blackness of their eyes. We both could feel it. We turned to run down the hallway then stopped when we saw two more of the children, salivating and trembling at the idea of having us cornered. The other two Blake had torn off of me were also slowly advancing.

But it was the octopus I was most scared of. It roared and gurgled, its gross arms writhing and swelling over itself in grotesque gray waves only to reveal two jet-black eyes staring up at us.

"Oh, no," I said. Without thinking, I slipped my hand into Blake's and held it tightly. I leaned back and felt him pull me closer. "I couldn't wait for Aunt Astrid and Bea. If I did, these things would have killed you. But because I couldn't wait for them, we couldn't finish the ritual, and we couldn't stop this thing, and now we're going to die anyways."

"I don't plan on going just yet." Blake pulled me into him with one arm and opened fire into the creature, blinding one of its eyes with a bullet right through the middle. Then he turned and aimed at the children that weren't really children and pulled the trigger.

Click! Click! Empty.

"Get ready to run!" he said.

"Run? Run where?"

"Run there!" He pointed past the children and down the stairs.

We'll never make it. Those things would latch onto us as if they were leeches, and that would be the end of it.

"One!" Blake shouted. "Two! Three!"

Just then, the front doors blew open with such force that the heavy wooden doors came off their hinges. Within seconds, I saw three dark figures and was sure they were the things lurking around in the woods that I had felt watching me as I'd made my way inside.

But then I heard a sound so familiar, I didn't think a choir of angels could have sounded so sweet.

"I will devour an entire feast! Let me start with this here beast!" The tiny spark swirling through the air got larger and larger, lighting up my Aunt Astrid, Bea, and Jake, as well as our trusty feline companions.

"The cavalry!" I screamed, nearly crying with happiness.

"What the hell is going on?" I could feel Blake's hand trembling in mine.

Jake opened fire and also wounded two of the creature's dozens of arms, making all of them recoil into themselves and slither back out in another direction.

The tentacles that had been whipping around in a wild fury of anger, searching out the assailants that had dared cause it pain, had now slowed to an almost glacial pace. Aunt Astrid had used a simple spell that many witches had used throughout history to slow down a chicken or turkey in order to catch it and kill it for dinner.

One witch could slow down a turkey on her own. It took my aunt, Bea, and the cats to overcome this monstrous creature. The thing tried to flip over and maneuver its good eye into a position to see who had barged in and was causing its victims to get away.

The one remaining black eye seared into my family, and within seconds, those creepy children were inching their way toward them. The long, gross arms of the octopus tried to roll after us, but they were getting tangled and knotted around each other, clumsily feeling their way, hoping to latch onto a human appendage. For a second, it reminded me of how I had talked after getting a mouth full of Novocain at the dentist.

"Come on!" Jake yelled. "Run!"

I tightened my grip on Blake's hand and pulled him toward the flashlight, down the stairs, and into our witches' circle. He was limping badly. I could only imagine what his leg looked like, but I could see the dark patches of blood that had soaked through his pant leg.

Treacle jumped up onto my shoulder and perched himself there, hissing at the children as they clawed and scraped their way toward us.

"They'll stop," Treacle said. *"They have a fear of cats."* He hissed wildly.

"How do you know that?"

"Because they tried to get in at the café. I thought you

knew that. These guys will tear apart a dog or boil a fish in its bowl. But cats freak them out. Watch this."

Treacle swiped his paw at them from several feet away.

The children froze in their tracks, their mouths pulled down in angry, terrified grimaces. Their hands clenched and unclenched, and they hissed back but made no attempt to come any closer.

Marshmallow and Peanut Butter were doing the same thing in the other directions, keeping those hateful siblings confined to the shadows, crying and hissing as if they were... well, a bunch of spoiled brats.

"Are we ready?" Jake yelled, watching behind them out the open door with his gun and flashlight raised.

My aunt and cousin and I all yelled at the same time, "Yes!"

Jake took Bea's hand. I grabbed Blake with Treacle still around my shoulders. Aunt Astrid kept the fireball burning overhead as she backed out with Marshmallow and Peanut Butter flanking her on either side.

As soon as she set foot on the front stoop, she waved her arms, and the doors flew back into position, wedging themselves into the doorframe. It would take the Jaws of Life to pry them open again.

The angry, loathsome sound of the children could still be heard outside as they scratched at the door with their little hands. They screamed and cried, but it was the grotesque rolling and slithering of those tentacles that stayed with me. They beat uselessly against the door.

All of us took off running down the cobblestone driveway.

"Why didn't you park closer?" I yelled while gasping for air.

"Are you kidding?" Bea yelled, her own breath coming out in bursts.

"If you'd like, you can walk!" Jake added.

"Maybe it's because two numbskulls parked and blocked the gate!" Aunt Astrid said, keeping up with the pack but bringing up the rear.

I was smiling. The cool air, the sound of crickets, and my whole family together, running for our lives. This was living.

Finally, we reached all our vehicles and stopped, panting and doubling over to get more of the sweet, cool air into our lungs.

"We'll meet you at home, young lady." My aunt

took my chin in her hand and looked me straight in the eye.

"What about the house? Do we need to take care of anything before we go?" I wanted to help. It was my attempt to fix what I had ruined. The ritual would have to be started over. What should have taken three days would now take six.

"We've got a binding spell on it," Bea said. "But one of us will have to come by and check on it every couple of hours to make sure there are no leaks or cracks." Bea held the door open for her mom and their two cats to climb into the back seat.

"I'll do that." I wiped the sweat from my brow. "I can totally do that."

"I know you will," my aunt said. Her face wasn't mean or angry, but it wasn't happy either.

Jake patted Blake on the back. "You okay to drive?" he asked as if this were no different than stopping someone with an expired license plate.

"I think so. I... Jake?"

"I don't know what to tell you, Blake. I'm just going to say get some rest and see how you feel in the morning. We'll talk then."

With that, Jake climbed into the driver's seat of his car and drove my family back in the direction of home.

I looked at Blake and noticed he wasn't looking at me. In fact, he was backing away from me.

"Do you want me to take a look at your leg?" I offered. "I might have some BAND-AIDs in my roadside first-aid box."

He shook his head as he backed up toward his car, looking down at the ground.

"I'm sorry I had to hit you," I said. "Maybe you'd like some ice or something?"

"I don't need any ice." He kept backing up, feeling along his car for the door handle as if he were afraid to turn his back on me. Like I might jump him or something.

"It's okay, Blake. Those things... well... they won't be able to get out and..."

"You need to move your car."

I stood there for a second, then I smiled as best I could. "Hey, I know it's kind of overwhelming, but there is an explanation for all this. If you'll just give me a couple minutes—"

"Move your car, Cath." He yanked the door open, climbed behind the steering wheel of his vehicle, and slammed the door shut. Then I heard him lock the doors.

Treacle, who had jumped off my shoulder while we were running, looked up at me from where he was sitting at my feet. When I opened my car door, he jumped right in and took his place on the passenger seat.

I swallowed hard, started the car, and slowly backed down the driveway. I pulled out onto the street and put my car in park, waiting for Blake to pull up next to me. But he sped out of the driveway without stopping.

Sitting there with the engine idling, I couldn't understand what had just happened. Didn't I save his life?

Treacle didn't purr. He didn't head butt me or meow. Instead, he just placed a paw on my thigh. His little gesture of kindness was probably the only one I was going to get from anyone for quite a while. I started to cry.

Trellis

bout a week had passed since the incident at the house.

The first few days had been very rough. I had stopped by the house on Butternut about six or seven times a day. Each time, I found a weak spot where those things were working to push their way through back into the outside world. I wore the amulet my mother had worn, to which my aunt had added a little extra power, and I also brought Treacle.

"I hate to punish you for what I did, Tre. But without doing anything, you keep these things scared and away while I fix any breaches."

"Do you really think hanging out on this beautiful bit of property is punishment?" Treacle asked. *"Are you kidding? In addition to the scratching and gnawing of those things*

you're keeping in there, I can hear the mice in the woods. Want to come with me and find a few?"

"Yeah, sure. Just let me finish checking the place and... oh, those rotten things!" I looked up and saw they had either chewed or scratched through a piece of the protection spell that was up at the roof. *"I can't get a break. Do you think there's a ladder around somewhere?"*

"No. But I'll bet you could climb that trellis."

The old, worn slats of the wooden trellis had dried snakes of ivy grown up and down on it, but it looked as though it were my only option.

Muttering to myself, I carefully climbed up the side of the building as Treacle jumped and stepped easily from ledge to ledge, light as a feather and as graceful as, well, as a cat.

I made it to the part that was damaged. Taking my amulet and a few special herbs Bea had given me, I whispered a quick reconstruction spell that sealed the opening and smoothed out the ridges. A few more steps up, and I was on part of the roof. I sat up there, letting my feet dangle over the edge.

"It's pretty up here," I said.

"Yes, but the mice are down there."

"You can go ahead, Treacle. I'm okay to just sit for a while."

Without a look back, my feline jumped from the

roof to a ledge then to a nearby branch, where he padded his way down in a zigzag fashion from branch to lower branch until he reached the ground.

It didn't take him long to head off into the woods, gingerly stepping over crunchy fallen leaves and barely making a sound.

Meanwhile, I looked around the area and noted the difference in the air. Whatever was inside the house had grown tired of fighting and was resting at the moment. Those black-eyed children were probably the ones trying to break through the spell since the damage looked a lot like what had been done at our houses. I thought if a giant octopus had been rolling down the streets, we would have heard about it by now.

My body ached, but I felt comfortable, up away from everything. It was better to be alone at the moment so I could get my head on straight and figure out my next step in whatever it was I was going to do.

I looked around while I was on the roof to see if I had missed anything. The repairs required a few different spells, and they had to be stronger and stronger each time. Exerting that kind of energy over and over for a couple of days had made me feel as though I were coming down with the flu. My body ached, my head wouldn't focus, and every bone screamed just to lie down for a month or two and rest.

But I knew it was my penance.

Aunt Astrid had said, "I'm sorry, Cath. I know you meant well, but what would have happened if we hadn't reached you in time? We had no idea if any of those quick-fix spells would work. Lucky for you, they did."

"What was I supposed to do? If I hadn't gotten there, Blake would have been hanging from the rafters by his neck. He had a rope and was crying. Aunt Astrid, I stood by while my mom got pulled under my bed. I didn't even reach out for her. I was too scared to do anything." I sniffed back the tears.

"Those festering talons reached out and latched onto her, digging their nails into her skin, pulling her while she screamed for help, all the while leaving a trail of blood along the floor. When all was said and done, that little bit of blood was all that was left of her because I was too scared to reach out a hand."

"Cath, you were only eleven years old. You couldn't help if you had wanted to."

"And then I saw the cats hanging and... never mind."

"What, honey?" My aunt took my hands in hers.

"You were tending to Bea. She had almost killed herself, thinking she saw Jake in that hole, and when we made our way out of that terrible place, I saw..."

"You saw what?"

"I saw all the cats. They had been tortured and killed, hanging by their necks from the trees. And a man. It was him. Had I let Blake do it, someone or something would have gotten to the cats too, right? That's what that means."

My aunt shook her head, looking at me with sad eyes. "Cath, why didn't you tell me what you saw?"

"You were busy with Bea."

"No." She seemed even more mad about this than she did that I'd ruined the ritual. "Do you think I see you as separate from her? That I would choose her well-being over yours because she is my daughter?"

I was ashamed of myself for feeling jealous of my cousin and best friend. I didn't say it out loud, but I had a feeling the tears in my eyes said it all.

"Cath, you and Bea are so different from each other. But I see you both as my girls. The loves of my life. Don't you know that?"

I nodded and shrugged. "She was so bad off in that place, though. I didn't want to act like I couldn't handle what had happened."

"And that is one of the beautiful things that sets you two apart." Taking both my hands in hers, she looked off behind me as she often did when she spoke, looking into the other dimensions and places in time.

"When Bea was a baby, she was so small. No smaller than a normal baby, but she was just always rolled up into a little butterball. And then you came along. Don't get me wrong. You were a butterball too. In fact, I think it has only been just recently that you've slowed down your eating habits since then. But you reached those pudgy hands out to everything. It didn't matter what it was. You were willing to risk a burn or two on the stove just to find out what someone else's definition of hot was."

I looked down in embarrassment. Baby stories were nice for other people, but I found them awkward.

"You don't like to hear about these things," my aunt said.

I shrugged.

"Too bad. You've been this way since you were born. Different. Independent. Let's face it. You're tough. But Cath, don't ever think you are so tough that you don't need your family. It may be twenty years before you have to call on us again. But we may need to call on you before then. It's your strength we needed for that ritual. I can't say what you did was wrong, running out there to help a man you care for. But it was reckless, and now you need to fix it."

"I will," I said. "I'll make it right."

"I know you will. And when your bones ache and your head throbs, just remember it's the price of caring for someone. I should know."

Bea was a lot more sympathetic. "You know, I would have done the same thing if it were Jake. Not a second thought to anyone or anything else. I'd be getting the same punishment as you, but don't think for a second I don't understand."

"I just couldn't leave him, knowing what those things do to a person," I said, almost ashamed. "If only he knew."

"He does." Bea rubbed my hands as we sat in her kitchen before walking to work together. "But you and I have grown up with that other world constantly knocking on our windows and doors. He's grown up thinking it was all make-believe. You can't expect him to just say, 'Okay. Witches and monsters and little devil children on a regular basis? Sign me up.'"

I tried to laugh, but it hurt to get it out. "He

didn't even try to talk to me. He sped out of there as if he owed me money or something."

"Just give it some time, Cath. You know how the universe has a way of bringing everything around the way it should be. Blake is an inquisitive man. Sooner or later, he's going to have to start asking questions. When he does, Jake won't be able to answer them. And I just won't. He'll have to come to you. He'll *want* to."

Treacle's Gift

❦

I saw Treacle appear again from the woods. He had a pep in his step, and his head was hanging low. Squinting, I could see why. At the edge of the wooded area, he stopped and sat with a dead mouse in his mouth. Dropping it in front of him, he gave a loud and proud meow.

"For me?" I asked him from the roof.

"I thought you could use a surprise," he said, licking his paw and looking up at me proudly.

Carefully, I climbed down off the roof the way I had come. The house was in good shape, and I wouldn't have much more of this before my aunt, Bea, and I put the final nail in the coffin. Getting the ritual done would lock those things up for good.

I walked over to Treacle slowly. *"Wow, buddy. That is a big one,"* I praised, picking it up by its tail.

"You'll eat it for lunch tomorrow?" he asked happily.

"Of course. Don't I always?"

Just because we could speak to each other didn't mean that Treacle stopped being a cat or stopped doing cat things. This dead mouse was the most precious gift because Treacle had gotten it especially for me.

Just like every parent worth their salt loved the crooked scribble-scrabble artwork their kids gave them over the years as if they had just replicated the Sistine Chapel, I loved Treacle's gifts too.

And just like parents who told their children about Santa Claus, I would continue to "eat these mice for lunch" when Treacle wasn't around because it made him happy, and I loved him.

I picked the dead thing up by the tail, holding back the shivers that rippled over my body every time I did this, and we made our way back to our car.

"If it were warmer out, I would have found you a snake."

"A snake? I don't think I've ever had one of those."

"They aren't the greatest, but sometimes you just want something crunchy."

"Yeah, I know what you mean, pal."

A FEW DAYS HAD PASSED SINCE THE WHOLE Butternut incident, as it had become known. Things in the town went on as normal.

Halloween was on a deliciously cloudy day that gave the whole town the appearance of an old Bela Lugosi film.

The children were all dressed up as the latest cartoon princess or superhero. And there were always those rebels we loved who made their own costumes. We had a cyborg cowboy, a bag of jelly beans, two pirates, and an old-fashioned ghoul minus all the blood and splatter so many of the kids liked these days.

When they stopped in the café, the kids were treated to hot apple cider and of course a big handful of what seemed like a bottomless pit of candy.

Truth be told, it sort of was bottomless since Aunt Astrid and Marshmallow had whispered a copying spell over the first three bags that were poured into our plastic jack-o-lantern bowl. Like the brooms and buckets of water in that Mickey Mouse movie, it just kept filling itself with every handful that was scooped out.

Later that night, the adults came out, asking for bottle caps or burned-out light bulbs for their grown-up scavenger hunts while yelling trick-or-treat as they entered and exited the café.

Bea was dressed in a fifties-style dress with pumps and a plastic hatchet in her head. "I'm June Cleaver," she would say, smiling like an angel while pointing to the cleaver in her head.

Jake came in wearing a cardigan sweater over a button-down white shirt and tan trousers with the same instrument in his head.

"Let me guess," I said, shaking my head. "Ward Cleaver."

"You're so perceptive, Cath," he teased. "What's the matter? Not in the holiday spirit?"

"What are you talking about? I'm wearing my costume." I was wearing an old pair of faded blue jeans and a black T-shirt with the word "Boo" written across the front.

"Well, you're wearing your mask, at least."

"Don't you ever get tired of saying that one, Jake?"

"Am I that predictable?"

I nodded, barely cracking a smile. Since Jake was like my brother-in-law, I took his ribbing and kind of enjoyed it. But that night, I just wasn't in the mood.

He slipped his arm around my shoulder and pulled me close to him. "I don't like this, Cath. You haven't been the same since that whole incident at the house. Are you all right?"

"Oh, yeah," I lied. "Sometimes that stuff just takes a lot out of a person. I'll be right as rain in the next couple of days. I promise."

"Well, you let me know if there's anything I can do for you. Sometimes a big brother can be helpful too, you know."

"Yeah, I know." I swallowed hard as I felt Jake's eyes still studying me as if I were a suspect in a crime.

I looked at a group of little kids that came carefully through the door. Of course, June Cleaver was happy to greet them with her big bowl of candy and gaping head wound. The funny thing was all the kids would leave with smiles and waves after they saw how much candy the crazy lady with the cleaver in her head was giving out.

"What do you hear from Blake? How's he doing?" I don't know where those words came from. They spilled out of my mouth as if I had no teeth and had tried to drink water.

"He's coming around. We've had some talks, but

until he really asks the hard questions, I can't push him. He's got to come around on his own."

Jake said that Blake had called in sick for the past couple of days. He had gone to talk to him, and I guess things were okay between the two of them. Men were weird that way. They could overlook and even accept the most blatant faults in each other. But Jake did say Blake wouldn't be coming by the house for a while.

By that time, my aunt, who was dressed like a gypsy, had come to join the conversation. "Is he quitting, Jake?" she asked, pouring Jake a to-go cup of coffee. I pretended not to have an interest in their conversation.

"I don't think so. He's a great detective, but openings are hard to come by. And he'd also have to start all over again if he decided to leave. Besides, he's not the kind of guy to leave a job unfinished." Jake tipped the cup to my aunt and kissed Bea good-bye.

"See you later, Cath. You coming for dinner tonight?"

"Later, Jake. Um, maybe." I couldn't even eat. I was barely able to finish my second hamburger from Wendy's that I had gotten for breakfast that morning.

I quickly turned away from my aunt and cousin as I wiped down the tables.

"Cath, are you okay?" my aunt asked.

I turned to look at her and felt the sting of tears in my eyes. I tried to bite my tongue like I used to in school so I wouldn't cry. But it wasn't working this time. Nodding, I let my hair fall in front of my face, hoping they wouldn't see I was upset.

"Yeah, I'm fine." It wasn't hard for me to feel their eyes on me. So I slowly turned around, looking everywhere but at their faces and shrugged.

"Give him time, Cath," Bea said, coming around the counter to hug me. I knew what she was doing. Her empathic abilities allowed her to ease the pain of a broken heart, but I took her hands and held her at bay.

"Keep your strength," I said, smiling. "I'm not that bad off."

"You are more important to him than you know," Bea said. "But a giant octopus coming out of the floor is enough to make even the most solid relationship feel wobbly."

Just then, my aunt let out a gasp. She was looking at something in front of the store on the sidewalk.

Both Bea and I turned to see Darla, walking and

smiling in an expensive fall outfit that made her look as pretty as the trees in their fall hues.

With her was a very dapper-looking Blake Samberg, who was grinning as he looked down, watching his feet take step after step, holding Darla's arm that was linked like a hook around his elbow.

I swallowed hard, then I took a deep breath and let it out.

About the Author

Harper Lin is the *USA TODAY* bestselling author of 6 cozy mystery series including *The Patisserie Mysteries* and *The Cape Bay Cafe Mysteries*.

When she's not reading or writing mysteries, she loves going to yoga classes, hiking, and hanging out with her family and friends.

For a complete list of her books by series, visit her website.

www.HarperLin.com